THE KING'S DAUGHTER

The King's Daughter

SUZANNE MARTEL

Revised Edition

A GROUNDWOOD BOOK
Douglas & McIntyre
Toronto Vancouver Buffalo

First published in French by Editions Fides under the title
Jeanne, fille du roy, copyright © 1974 by Suzanne Martel
English translation copyright © 1980 by Groundwood Books
Revised edition copyright © 1994 by Groundwood Books
Third printing 2000

Groundwood Books / Douglas & McIntyre Ltd.
720 Bathurst Street, Suite 500, Toronto, Ontario M5S 2R4

Distributed in the U.S.A. by Publishers Group West
1700 Fourth Street, Berkeley, CA 94710

We acknowledge the support of the Canada Council for the Arts and the
Ontario Arts Council for our publishing program.

Canadian Cataloguing in Publication Data

Martel, Suzanne, 1924-
[Jeanne, fille du roy. English]
The king's daughter
Rev. ed.
Translation of : Jeanne, fille du roy.
ISBN 0-88899-323-4 (bound) ISBN 0-88899-218-1 (pbk.)
I. Title. II. Title: Jeanne, fille du roy. English.
PS8526.A726J4213   jC843'.54   C94-932549-X
PZ7.M37Ki 1994

Cover art by Harvey Chan
Book design by Michel Solomon
Printed and bound in Canada

*To Suzanne and Luc,
who could have been
Jeanne and Simon*

1

"A KING'S daughter! I'm a king's daughter!"

Closing the parlour door without a sound, as she had been taught, Jeanne repeated the magic words that had just changed her life. Her heart was beating wildly. She pressed both hands to her chest as her thin face relaxed into an unguarded smile.

As for Mother Superior de Chablais, she breathed a sigh of relief. Sitting across from her in the dim parlour with the rows of straight, unfriendly chairs, her visitor, Marguerite Bourgeoys, looked at her indulgently. A wise woman, she had read the very different thoughts running through the nun's mind and through that of her student. With the burning energy of an eighteen-year-old, Jeanne Chatel was trembling with joy under her submissive, reserved appearance.

"Of course, madame. If my mother superior gives me her permission, I will go to New France. No, madame. I have no fear. I am strong and the risk does not frighten me."

Not as much as the prospect of life in a convent, Marguerite Bourgeoys concluded to herself. Here's a swallow who doesn't appreciate her cage, and I'm setting her free.

So the fate of this poor orphan was decided at last; her noisy and prolonged stay had upset the peaceful rhythm of monastic life. The king would supply the dowry, the convent the orphan, and the distant colony would be richer by one new bride. Each would be delighted, Mother de Chablais most of all, for she could finally devote herself entirely to the education of more docile subjects.

In a word, Jeanne Chatel was the ordeal of the Daughters of the Congregation. She had come to them at the age of ten, small and undernourished, almost wild, and in open revolt against the universe.

Raised in a tumble-down house by her recluse grandfather, who was a bit of a poacher, the little girl had lost the protector she adored and the wild freedom in which she had grown up—both at the same time.

For two days she had hidden at the back of a closet like a wounded animal. Neither the compassionate nuns' pleading nor the indignant Mother Superior's threats had made her come forth from her hiding place.

Finally, chasing everyone away, an old nun took the situation in hand. Armed with patience and a delicious-smelling apple tart, the convent cook, Sister Berthelet, sat down in front of the fugitive's hiding place and waited with the tenacity of a hunter lying in wait for his prey.

Soon a slight rustling and a covetous sigh rewarded her perseverance. A brown head that had never known a comb appeared in the doorway. A dirty, pitifully thin hand reached for the tempting dish. Without a word, the nun offered the tart and the starving little girl devoured it, squatting at the feet of her protectress. The sister caressed the little girl's tangled hair with a reassuring hand and murmured comforting words.

Jeanne put the empty plate on the floor and raised her

frightened eyes. She read so much compassion in that wrinkled face that, with a cry of despair, she threw herself into the outstretched arms. For the first time since her grandfather's death, the orphan burst into tears.

Mother de Chablais found her new charge asleep in Sister Berthelet's arms. Her dirty cheeks streaked with tears, her hand desperately clutching the nun's wrinkled coif, Jeanne was still shaken by sighs.

"She's a poor unfortunate little bird," the old woman explained. "She's going to find convent life hard."

"Nevertheless, she'll have to adjust to it, sister. It's the fate of all orphans."

The friendship that bound the wild little girl and the woman stooped with age eased Jeanne's difficult period of adaptation to the ordered existence of the convent school. The entire order set about the task of "taming" Jeanne Chatel.

That task did not go smoothly, or without Homeric fits of anger and vehement protestations. The rebel did not understand why it was necessary to brush her hair, wash her hands and curtsey.

If Jeanne's education had presented problems, her schooling brought some surprises. The little girl read fluently and wrote with the mastery of a clerk. During the long winter evenings by the hearth in the large, dark room—the sole remains of what had once been the fine family home—her learned grandfather had enjoyed transmitting his knowledge to this intelligent, bright child. Greek and Latin poets, the classics of the time, world history, the rudiments of arithmetic—all these had been absorbed pell-mell and made for an astonishing and rather disturbing hodgepodge.

On the other hand, a complete ignorance of the shorter catechism, basic prayers and the meaning of the religious services provided the scandalized nuns with a vast field of soul-saving action.

After eight years, by sheer force of patience, kindness and firmness—and thanks to Sister Berthelet's instinctive psychology—they managed to make the wild little girl into a very presentable student...on the surface. Alas! the veneer was thin. Her stormy temperament, the inheritance of a vindictive grandfather, was always smouldering under her compliant appearance.

Jeanne had no home other than the convent that had sheltered her, no family other than the nuns and no future other than to enter the sisterhood. She had not yet been able to resign herself to that final commitment, the normal fate of girls without a dowry. It seemed to her a great injustice not to feel it was her vocation, and she took herself to task for it, as if it were a failing in her.

Her friends Geneviève, Anne and Marie, serene and self-effacing, glided smoothly towards the religious life. But why this feeling of revolt, this taste for flight when, above the grey walls of the convent, she saw the smoke of the peaceful chimneys of the little town of Troyes? Some of her companions would escape to marry a distant cousin, a widower burdened with children, or a rich old man who would forego the dowry for the freshness of an eighteen-year-old.

Even this sad choice was not open to Jeanne. She had to admit that, in the eyes of the nuns, her education was a fiasco. She really could not be recommended as a model wife. She burned the pastry, forgot to put on her cap, galloped

through the halls, bounded down the stairs, and her prover-
bial carelessness was not even redeemed by a befitting
sweetness.

Still, leaning against the parlour door, Jeanne was dreaming, though wide awake. How right she had been to hope,
to believe that in spite of everything life had some joy and
surprises in store for her! Only now did she dare acknowledge what tenacious hopes had kept her from yielding to all
the pressure and had made her put off her inevitable entry
into the convent from one season to the next. Never had a
way of life seemed so unnatural to the one contemplating it.

When her protectress, Sister Berthelet, died quietly one
summer morning the previous year, Jeanne had felt she was
losing her grandfather all over again. Since that day, no one
had considered her boisterous gaiety and her liveliness as
good qualities. On the contrary, they held them against
her—just as they did her alluring bosom and her unruly
hair that escaped in curls from under her severe cap. So
much vitality was a little frightening to the nuns; they had
fled just these excesses by taking refuge in the convent.
Jeanne strove towards a sense of balance, hoping one day it
would actually sink in.

But now all that was in the past. What a glorious future
was opening up before her, an orphan! Sister Bourgeoys's
warnings did not even reach her buzzing ears.

Already she saw "adventure"—a tall sailing ship, the
boundless sea, the magnificent, primitive continent, a vigorous colony waiting just for Jeanne Chatel so it could pros-
per and spring into action. She would be as courageous and
bold as the gallant knights in the novels in her grandfather's
library.

Jeanne had but one regret. Alas! never again would her personal gallant knight, the handsome Thierry de Villebrand, be able to find her to carry her off on his great white steed.

With all the wisdom of her eighteen years, Jeanne had to admit that, since he knew where she was, her hero could have come to fetch her long ago. Their last meeting, when she was ten years old and dared throw a handful of mustard in his eyes, hardly lent itself to demonstrations of sentimentality. Who cares? The devil with fantasies! Hurray for today's fine reality! Instead of an imaginary character she had invented to fill her youthful dreams, drawing on two brief encounters with a handsome young man, she would have a husband of her own, a husband awaiting her this very moment upon the distant shores of New France.

"A king's daughter! I am a king's daughter!"

Against all the laws of propriety, Jeanne picked up her skirts in both hands and, two steps at a time, bounded up the long convent stairways leading to the attic. She burst into the garret she shared with three other orphans, brandishing her piece of paper.

"Ladies, I am a king's daughter off to New France. Here's the list of the trousseau we must prepare for my departure in June. Ladies, give me a curtsey, then get to work."

Anne and Geneviève abandoned the lace they were crocheting near the window by dusk's uncertain light. Younger than their roommate, the two orphans were filled with an admiration mixed with fear at Jeanne's bold acts.

They surrounded her, pestering her with a thousand questions.

"Is that why they wanted you in the parlour, and not

because of the bread you forgot in the oven?"

"Who cares? What's a miserable loaf of bread for a ward of Louis XIV? Don't bother me with those petty little problems anymore."

"But, Jeanne, aren't we all the king's daughters? Are you any more than we?"

Raised at the State's expense, the orphans were always reminded of their privileged status as wards of the Crown. The way Jeanne claimed this title, as if it were suddenly hers alone, intrigued Anne. In her naive mind she already pictured her friend at Versailles, among the ladies-in-waiting.

"I mean that our gracious sovereign will provide me with a dowry and a trousseau in a big trunk and send me over to New France to marry one of his loyal subjects."

"You're leaving us? Are you going to those far-off places?"

Anne was crushed and already mourning Jeanne's departure. Geneviève, more practical, consulted the list: "Two lace coifs, six linen caps, a blue wool skirt, a serge skirt, two white linen shirts, two pairs of white stockings, a petersham camisole, a piqué bodice, six cotton handkerchiefs, sheepskin gloves. That's much more than for entering the convent!"

"Obviously." Jeanne pirouetted, her arms high, her skirt swirling. "I'm crossing the ocean. I'm going to the ends of the earth. Just think. They say that in winter you can't see anything but snow for leagues around. Sister Marguerite Bourgeoys, Mother de Chablais's friend, will come with us to Ville-Marie where she has a school."

"Whom are you going to marry?" asked Anne anxiously.

"Probably a military man, perhaps a captain."

"Where will you live?"

13

"Anywhere but in a convent! In the town or in the garrison fort. Perhaps I am to accompany my husband to the governor's court."

Geneviève, always the realist, suggested, "And if your husband is a farmer?"

"Then we'll have cows and chickens and all the neighbours will come to visit."

Nothing could crush Jeanne's optimism.

Timidly Anne asked, "And Lord Villebrand whom you've been waiting for for eight years...what will he say about your departure?"

Jeanne would keep her companions in suspense with impassioned tales of her adventures with the handsome Thierry. He had come alive from one story to the next, so much so that all her confidantes believed in him.

She answered flippantly, "He need only have come before. You can wait for a white horse for eight years. Longer than that is too much."

"Oh, I thought it was the lord you were waiting for, not the horse," teased Geneviève. She, too, was going to miss their companion's exciting stories.

A discreet knock at the door interrupted the three friends' conversation. Marie du Voyer, the fourth occupant of the room, stood in the doorway, blonde and blushing, a letter pressed to her heart.

"Jeanne, I'll be leaving with the king's daughters, too, and..." With a trembling hand she held out an envelope to her friend. "I've received an offer of marriage."

The crumpled yellowed letter, already a year old, had travelled far. It came from Monsieur Simon de Rouville, a distant relative of her father, who had settled in Ville-Marie.

His wife and one son had been killed by the Iroquois, and he was left with two young children. He had remembered his cousin's poor orphaned daughter; would she come to New France to be his wife?

"But," objected Anne, "I thought you wanted to enter the convent..."

"Our Mother Superior thinks, as I do, that my duty is over there," Marie murmured.

Jeanne put the letter back in the envelope, thinking to herself, Still another whose vocation is a necessity. Poor girl, how unromantic. That Monsieur de Rouville wants a housekeeper and he's making no secret of it.

And in her galloping imagination, she pictured her own very uncertain future: the handsome military man who would command a detachment on the wharf as the boat landed; their eyes would meet...understandingly. Or the gallant lord who would offer her holy water after the service. Their eyes would meet...he would be the one. What difference did it make? Jeanne knew, wanted to know but one thing. Her prison door was opening, the great adventure was beginning.

2

THAT evening as usual, after the prayers were said and the candle blown out, the confabulations began in the attic room. A ray of moonlight silvered the four narrow beds standing side by side.

Jeanne, draped in her voluminous nightdress, went to the window. How she loved the still of the night! In her heart this orphan girl still longed for her almost unfettered youth.

It was on moonlit evenings like this one that her grandfather would take her through Lord Villebrand's woods to set his snares. At his side she had learned not to fear the nocturnal rustlings of the forest and to glide like a shadow through the mysterious trees. The learned man would explain the solar system, the rotation of the earth and the names of the stars.

Before dawn they would return along shadowy paths, hand in hand, the fruit of their larceny tucked away in the game sack. In his fine deep voice, her grandfather would recite one of Villon's poems or Horace's odes. Through the comforting magic of his presence, the night became a friendly refuge. The same magic of their love for one another made the half-charred ruins of the house a happy home for Jeanne, the only one she had known, though the inhabitants of the area maintained it was haunted and avoided it fearfully. Her mother had died when she was born and her father a month later. Honoré Chatel took in his grand-daughter, the child of his only son, and brought her to his lair, all that remained of a once prosperous estate adjacent to Lord Villebrand's land.

The Chatel family, who belonged to the gentry, had been dishonoured and ruined by an ancestor who had fall-en into disgrace with a spiteful king. The slander of a pow-erful and jealous neighbour, a Count de Villebrand, had been at the origin of this disaster. Little by little the land, then the personal effects, jewels, books, furniture—every-thing had been sold. Finally a fire destroyed the house; only its large living room was spared. Jeanne grew up in those dismal surroundings, knowing cold and hunger but sur-rounded by love. She lived a strange existence, divided between life's harsh realities and the fantastic and imaginary world her grandfather recreated for her through his stories and books.

Jeanne had done the same for her friends, bringing the only fantasy into their ordered, monotonous life, conjuring up for them the magic hours and the legends that had enchanted her childhood.

That evening they learned she was soon to depart. As if to reassure themselves, her friends begged her, as they often did, to "tell us about Thierry."

Sometimes Jeanne would refuse, regaling them instead with stories of knights drawn straight from her varied reper-toire, or with the exciting adventures of the gods of Greek mythology.

But the moon was shining in the Troyes sky, Jeanne was

in high spirits, and she agreed to launch into her most beautiful story: the one that was almost true.

"This will be the last time I'll tell it to you. Now we know the ending, and it won't be the one we'd dreamed of."

Marie, Anne and Geneviève held their breath while their friend collected her thoughts. In a low voice full of mystery, Jeanne began.

"When I climbed to the very top of the big oak tree, I would see the towers of the Villebrand chateau. I knew that there lived the lord whose grandfather had ruined my ancestor. And I used to say to myself that one day I would be the Countess of Villebrand and avenge my family."

The storyteller's friends shivered deliciously.

"One day, when I was eight years old, I went to steal nuts in the part of the estate that was near our house. To do that, I had to jump over an old stone wall with iron pickets on top."

"How high was the wall?" asked Geneviève. She had known the answer for years but asked again every time.

"Higher than the convent wall. Too high to get over easily. I had to climb a tree whose branches drooped over the top of the wall. From there I let myself hang from my arms, then I jumped to the ground and rolled."

The orphans, who were forbidden to go up the stairs two at a time, had unabashed admiration for the storyteller's boldness.

"Weren't you afraid?" Anne asked timidly for the hundredth time.

"Not at all. I'd been doing that since I was six."

Jeanne was patient with the interruptions; for her companions they were part of the story. She continued, "That time I tried to jump too soon. I was left hanging by my skirt on one of the pickets on the top. I was hanging like a picture on a wall, struggling to get back up, when I heard ferocious barking that was coming closer. I knew there were guard dogs on the Villebrand estate, but they never went far from the chateau, and I'd never seen them near the wall."

"Were you afraid?" Marie trembled with sympathetic fear.

"I was more afraid of being caught. Going onto an estate without permission is serious. Before I was able to unhook myself, two big angry dogs charged out of the woods and jumped at me, growling."

Jeanne pictured herself again, bending her knees, kicking her feet to escape the threatening fangs, desperately trying to slip her hand into her pocket.

"Why?" breathed Geneviève, for whom this gesture seemed the ultimate in composure. "What were you looking for in your pocket?"

"The bag of mustard powder that Grandfather always made me carry to protect myself against villains or wild animals."

Nothing seemed more adventurous to the breathless listeners than this need to be armed against such formidable dangers at the age of eight.

"Would you have really thrown mustard in the dogs' faces?"

"Of course. Especially since one of them had just torn open my calf with its claws. I was terrified. I thought I was done for."

"And just then..." Geneviève suggested, eyes wide.

"Just then I heard a horse galloping. A voice called out

sharply, 'Sultan, Dragon, come here.' The dogs turned and ran towards their master, tails between their legs."

"And what about you?"

"I was still hanging by my old skirt that should have torn but wouldn't let go. Blood was running down my foot."

"And then?"

This was the best part of the story, the one that made their romantic hearts beat faster.

"Then he came towards me. Thierry de Villebrand, the count's son, came to my aid."

"On his big white horse?"

"On his big white hunting horse. He came over to the wall and took a good long look at me."

"Was he handsome?" Anne sighed.

"As handsome as the statue of Saint Michael in the chapel. Tall, blond, tanned, dressed in buckskin and leather boots, with his hunting rifle over his shoulder."

"Was he old?"

That question was essential to the story. Jeanne had been waiting for it before continuing.

"He seemed old to me. He was fifteen."

"What did he do?"

"He said in a mocking voice, 'Only foolish little birds get caught in the net.'"

This unromantic remark nonetheless proved that noblemen are never at a loss for words.

"And what did you say?"

"What could I have said? I waited, hanging there foolishly while he went on laughing. He had very white teeth and his eyes were as blue as the sky."

Three sighs broke the silence.

Here the story became less enchanting, but only for an unpleasant moment that quickly passed. It seemed to the listeners that the heroine had not been true to her role. But it must not be forgotten that the heroine was Jeanne Chatel, hardly known for her patience.

"I got angry seeing him there, so conceited on his horse. I cried, 'If you came here just to watch me, you can leave. This is all I'm going to do.'"

Was that any way to talk to a handsome knight?

"Was he insulted?"

"No. But he stopped laughing and asked, 'Did you hurt yourself?'"

"I said, 'No, but your dogs hurt me.'"

"He saw the gash on my leg. Immediately he brought his horse very close to the wall, stood up in the stirrups and took me under the arms. He tried to unhook my skirt, but his horse was prancing and he didn't succeed. My old skirt was strong."

"What did he do?" Anne whispered wildly.

"He took his dagger from his boot and murmured, 'too bad.' Then he ripped the cloth right to the top and freed me."

"Did you fall to the ground?"

"No. He had a firm hold on me. I wasn't very big. Don't forget I was only eight years old."

Alas, they had forgotten!

"He seated me in front of his horse and said to me, 'I'm going to take you home. You can't walk with your leg like that.' Then he took a big white handkerchief from his pocket, folded it and bent down and put it around my calf that was bleeding and hurt very much.

"Then he prodded his horse into a walk and asked, 'Where do you live? In the village?'

"I said, 'No. I'm Jeanne Chatel. I live right by the estate, on the other side of the wall.'

"Since it wasn't his family that had been ruined, he had forgotten the story of the ancestors. He simply said, 'I'm Thierry de Villebrand.' Then he added, 'so you're the old recluse's granddaughter?'

"I didn't know what that word meant, but the expression seemed offensive to me. I retorted, 'My grandfather is an honest man.'

"He replied mockingly, 'As honest as his granddaughter who climbs walls to steal apples.'

"I was furious. Without thinking, I blurted out, 'I didn't want apples. I was looking for nuts. There aren't any apples near here.'

"He had a good laugh over my accidental confession. He said, 'Listen, if you want nuts, don't break your neck climbing over the wall. I'm going to show you a break I discovered when I was young. And near there is a wild apple tree nobody knows about. When I go back to school in Paris, the dogs won't come this way again. Take all the fruit you want and nobody will be the wiser.'"

"He was generous," Geneviève remarked.

"Perhaps he knew about the story of his ancestor, and he wanted to make up for the injustice," Anne suggested.

"Perhaps. I didn't ask him. I was happy enough to get out of it so well. He took a crust of bread from his pocket and offered it to me. I was hungry and I ate it. When we rode under the big oak tree I had climbed to see the chateau, Thierry said, 'When I was little, this tree was my sailing ship. I was her captain. I used to hide here to get away from my tutor. The view is very beautiful up there.'

"Before I knew it, I'd answered, 'I know. I often climb up there. It's my chateau.'

"He murmured, 'so, you search for happiness in dreams, too.' Then he didn't say anything more until we reached the house. Grandfather was on the doorstep. He was worried because night was falling. He recognized my saviour and frowned. Thierry greeted him courteously and, holding me by the wrists, helped me get down. Grandfather caught me in his arms.

"Thierry was very ill at ease and embarrassed. He took a silver coin from his pocket and offered it to me.

"'That's to replace your skirt I had to cut with my knife.'

"Not knowing what to do, I accepted the coin. Grandfather took it away from me and threw it at him, saying, 'the Chatels don't need charity from their more fortunate neighbours.'

"Thierry went red in the face. He turned his horse and left at a gallop, whistling for his dogs. I didn't see him again for two years."

"But you didn't forget him, did you?"

You'd think such a crime would have been inexcusable.

"Of course I thought of him every time I went through the hole in the wall and picked 'his' apples and 'his' nuts. And when I climbed up the old oak, I wondered which turret of the chateau his room was in."

"In the highest one, for sure," Geneviève stated with conviction.

3

AFTER a long silence in which each girl dreamed of her personal version of the adventure, Jeanne continued in a barely audible voice, for this part of the story still pained her, even after eight years.

"One evening, some time before Christmas, when I was ten years old, Grandfather came back from the forest, very pale and ill. The game wardens had chased him for a long time and he had had to run very fast. He lay down on his bench near the hearth and asked me to put a lot of logs on the fire. He was shivering. He slept a little, and later he asked me to light all the candles we owned. That surprised me, since we were always very sparing with light. Now I know Grandfather didn't want me to be afraid of death, all alone in the darkness. I thought it was a celebration. It was warm and bright in our house as never before."

Marie, Anne and Geneviève pictured an attractive, rustic cottage. Never had Jeanne been able to reconcile herself to giving a faithful description of the charred ruin that had been the centre of her happiness. Her friends couldn't see with her eyes that immense, desolate room, where tattered tapestries disguised the very tall windows with their permanently closed shutters. Candlelight flickered on the blackened beams of the ceiling, lending a sinister air to the only ancestral portrait to survive the disaster. The few remaining pieces of furniture and the bookshelves had been arranged around the fireplace, leaving the rest of the room empty but for the echoing footsteps. All of Jeanne Chatel's world was contained in those ten square feet of light and warmth.

"Then, calmly, as if he were telling me a story, Grandfather prepared me for his death. He had me lift a hearthstone; underneath it was a gold chain with a medal of the Virgin. In a new voice, very soft and slow, he said to me as he put the chain around my neck, 'tomorrow you will go and take this jewel to the priest, and you will tell him I want to be laid to rest with my ancestors in the cemetery. The medal will pay the cost of a service and everything else. Then you will go to Troyes and you will tell Madame de Chablais, the Mother Superior of the Congregation, that you are my granddaughter. I knew her well at one time. She will take you in.'

"It all seemed so easy and natural that I didn't think of being frightened. I thought it was one of Grandfather's new stories, and since he seemed tired, I didn't want to bother him with my objections. Tomorrow he would be better and would forget all that.

"Then he told me death was a rest in a garden of dreams. There you would find all those you had loved in life, even the dogs that had been your faithful friends. He promised me he would wait for me peacefully, smoking his pipe, setting his snares and fishing for trout in the forests of paradise. Then he told me, 'Go to bed, my darling. Tonight it's too cold to go poaching. Go to sleep. I am going to have a rest, and tomorrow you will remember my advice.'

"He kissed me on the forehead as he did every evening. I found it strange to sleep with all that light, but it was just those unexpected fancies that made life with my grandfather charming.

"I woke up very early because the fire had gone out. All the candles had burned their wicks right down. It was dark and I knew Grandfather was dead."

The three friends cried openly over this story. Though it had been repeated a hundred times, it was still moving. Jeanne envied them their soothing tears. Never had she been able to cry over this memory, perhaps because Honoré Chatel had succeeded so well in his mission to soften his death for his granddaughter.

In her even voice, Jeanne continued her story. "The priest accepted the medal. Women I didn't know forced me to wear black clothing that was too big for me. They didn't want me to enter the church where the service was taking place. They made me stay in one of their houses, in a dusty sitting room where they recited the rosary. I was certain that wasn't what Grandfather would have wanted. So I ran away."

"Where, Jeanne? Where could you go in the winter when you were ten?"

There was but one refuge, all four knew, but they had to ask the ritual questions.

"I fled to the Villebrand estate, through the hole in the wall, and I climbed up the oak, higher than ever. From there I saw them put Grandfather in a hole in the cemetery. Then they returned to their houses.

"Later they started searching for me. They ran to our house, towards the town, along the paths, calling me and promising me good things to eat.

"I was cold and hungry, but I knew that if I came down, they would shut me up in a convent. I preferred to die in my tree."

Do we need novels, Geneviève, Anne and Marie wondered, when we live with a real heroine?

Jeanne pictured herself again, huddled on a branch, paralyzed, her mind empty, oblivious to the weather and the cold, waiting, waiting.

The silence wore on. Anne took up the thread of the story again. "Then Thierry arrived on his big white horse."

"Yes. He had come from Paris to spend Christmas with his family. I saw him in the distance talking to the villagers who were pointing towards our house and waving their arms.

"Some time later, he stopped his horse at the foot of the oak and started to climb up to me through the branches. He said softly, 'I knew you'd be here in your chateau. Come down now. The time for dreams is over. Come, my poor little bird.'

"I was so frozen that my hands couldn't grip the branches. He carried me in his arms down to the foot of the tree."

"He was strong," said Anne dreamily.

"I wasn't heavy and I was only ten years old. He was already a man, very tall and strong."

The listeners were always being brutally brought back to reality. This romance existed only in their minds. The heroine was but a child.

"And he took you to the convent?"

"He was heading for Troyes, holding me firmly in front of him on his horse. I felt reassured. Suddenly I came back to my senses. I had to escape or be in prison for life."

"All the same, Jeanne, the convent isn't so terrible."

"I know now. At that time, it seemed like a fate worse than death. I decided to run away. I still had the bag of mustard powder I had been carrying around in vain all those years. I slipped my hand into my pocket and carefully stuck my fingers in the powder. I had taken a long time to decide and we were approaching the first houses in the town."

"And you did it? You dared to blind your benefactor?"

"In my eyes he wasn't my benefactor. I think I'd become a little mad from grief and fatigue. I turned around and, sharply, I threw the mustard in his face."

Sitting on their beds, Anne, Geneviève and Marie shuddered as they relived that heroic scene.

"You did dare, Jeanne, that's terrible. Was he furious?"

"He cried out and put his hands to his eyes. I was about to jump when he caught me by the shoulder and growled between clenched teeth, 'Silly little fool. You won't get away from me.'

"He didn't let me go. He threw back his head while tears ran from his reddened, closed eyes. He tried to rub his eyelids with his free hand. I felt him shaking against me. He took out his handkerchief, just like the one he'd given me the other time, and held it out to me with a trembling hand.

"'Quick, wet it with the water in my flask.' I emptied the water onto the handkerchief, then right onto his upturned face. He shook his head and clenched his teeth. He held the handkerchief up to his eyes and groped for the reins. The horse had come to a stop.

28

"I put them into his hand and he dug his heels into his mount. In a gasp he said, 'take me to the convent. I can't see anything. You burned my eyes!'

"I was terrified. I don't remember how we reached the convent.

"In front of the congregation gate I said to him, 'Here it is.' I'd already been by there with Grandfather, and he'd pointed out the windows with their opaque glass and the high, thick wall.

"Thierry let me slide to the ground, still holding me by the wrist. He had never once released me the entire time. He, too, jumped down blindly. He was holding the hand-kerchief to his eyes and staggering. I pulled him by the arm towards the front door. I rang, rang with all my might. When the nuns arrived, Thierry was kneeling on the ground, half unconscious. They carried him into the convent.

" 'What happened to you?' someone asked.

" 'It was an accident,' he murmured. 'I got something in my eye.' He didn't betray me, and they forgot all about me. I hid in a corner. Afterward I learned from Mother de Chablais that he never accused me. No one understood what had happened to him. They called Monseigneur de Villebrand from the archbishop's palace. He took his nephew to his house and they looked after him. After a few days he was cured, so they said, and he went back to Paris.

"During that time I was accepted into the congregation."

Geneviève and Anne, who had arrived at the convent at a very young age, were never told about the new boarder's stormy beginnings. And Jeanne didn't boast about it.

With her hands clasped, Anne murmured dreamily, "And then you received the letter..."

"Yes. I was given a missive, the first, the only one I've received in my life. It contained the chain and the gold medal I'd given the priest for Grandfather's funeral. Thierry must have bought them back."

"And what did the letter say?" asked Geneviève, who had read and reread the yellowed piece of paper her friend preciously kept in her cupboard, under the large white handkerchief embroidered with the Villebrand coat-of-arms.

As if she had the paper before her, Jeanne recited in the darkness, "It began with 'Mademoiselle Jeanne,' as if I was a real lady.

> *Mademoiselle Jeanne,*
> *Here is the medal that belonged to your family, that the priest gave me to pass on to you. Keep it in memory of your grandfather, and consider it a gesture of reparation for the wrongs my family has done to yours.*
> *I believe I understand now what impulse made you act as you did. I admire courage; that's why I will never forget yours. It will serve as an inspiration to me all my life.*
> *I hope that in time you will understand why I intervened, and that you will not hold it against me, as I do not blame you for your actions.*
> *Mademoiselle, I remain the most faithful and devoted of your servants,*
>
> *Thierry de Villebrand*

"How beautiful and how well written it is!" sighed Anne,

getting back into bed.

The true story ended there. The four friends had enjoyed adding various epilogues through the years, creating a legend of love around astonishing but plausible events. Now, all these romantic endings were no longer needed.

By agreeing to go to New France, Jeanne Chatel had moved from hypothetical legend to living adventure. She would be led to her destiny not by a big white horse, but by an even more picturesque sailing ship.

Anne and Geneviève, those docile, fearful future nuns, had no illusions about themselves. They admired their friend's courage, but nothing would induce them to go beyond the reassuring gates that would forever surround their peaceful existence. Without Jeanne's presence, Marie would never have dared face her new destiny, either.

The chapel clock softly sounded. Jeanne slid between the rough sheets, her eyes opened wide in the silvery night. She clasped the gold medal hanging around her neck and dreamed of the future.

4

LE HAVRE, July, 1672

"Cast off the moorings!" The cry was repeated, and the thick ropes were rolled up like sleeping serpents. The sailors clambered up into the rigging; the sails were unfurled and flapped in the wind.

Slowly the ship turned and slipped out to sea. On the wharf of Le Havre de Grace, the Normandy port from which they set sail, handkerchiefs were waved in farewell.

On the deck of the sailing ship, Sister Bourgeoys's orphans—six novices and five future brides—watched the shore grow distant. A young stranger waved his hat earnestly; Jeanne decided to imagine he was her despairing lover sending his final farewell to the king's daughter whose hand had been refused him.

After a long month's wait in Rouen while the boat was being prepared, the great departure day had finally dawned. Jeanne was leaving her country with no regret, but Marie was crying softly beside her, conscious only of a separation. She was moved by the grief of those among the forty-five passengers who were leaving a loved one behind on the shores of France.

Marie was holding tightly the letter that had changed her life. And Jeanne, her heart sinking, wondered if her very vulnerable friend would find the understanding husband she deserved in Monsieur de Rouville.

Jeanne felt directly concerned for her friend's happiness; that was part of clever Sister Berthelet's plans for adapting the girls to convent life. She gave an older girl the responsibility for a younger incoming one who was lost and in distress. Marie du Voyer's parents had perished in a coach accident, and the eight-year-old orphan, blonde and timid, had been inconsolable.

Jeanne had been eleven years old—tall, sturdy and resourceful. The nun had brought Marie to her and said, "My child, there's someone here who needs you. She will be your little sister. Protect her, for it is in helping others that we know happiness."

Marie du Voyer blossomed under her new friend's energetic influence. Jostled and stimulated by Jeanne, she gave her the joys of sisterhood in return. The older girl had poured out all the unfulfilled tenderness of her solitary childhood onto that trusting child. Marie's gentleness had often calmed Jeanne, and many times Jeanne's boldness had given Marie courage, as on this departure day.

The sailors bustled about, orders were shouted back and forth, the passengers were excited. It was Sister Bourgeoys's fifth crossing, and she busied herself getting the trunks stored in the narrow, overcrowded cabins.

Jeanne, curious as usual, watched the manoeuvres with fascination. The sailors climbing up the rigging with the agility of monkeys reminded her of her own ascent into the oak tree of her childhood. How distant it was, her chateau in a tree! Somewhere, perhaps, Thierry had found the sailing ship of his dreams. Jeanne, watching as the shore disappeared on the horizon, bade farewell to her childhood and turned resolutely towards the future.

Leaning against the rail, Marie was still crying. Her impatient friend was about to give her a good scolding, when suddenly she stopped. An officer was circulating among the passengers, asking them to return to their cabins to facilitate the manoeuvres.

He approached the tearful young girl. Jeanne saw him bow and offer Marie first his handkerchief, then his arm.

From a distance, she discreetly watched the officer escorting the pretty blonde to the door of her cabin. When he returned to the deck and crossed paths with Jeanne, she noticed that he was young and handsome.

She found her friend Marie sitting on her trunk, hands clasped, eyes shining. Her intuition for romance told her—even before the victims knew—that here was a pair of bashful lovers.

Marie was holding the handkerchief between her fingers. Jeanne teased her gently, "It seems that handkerchiefs are going to play a big role in our lives."

"Of course, of course, Jeanne," Marie answered absently. She hadn't heard a thing her friend had said.

5

THE crossing was short for those times: it took forty-one days. Jeanne, forced into idleness and impatient for the future, found it long. But it lasted no more than an instant for Marie du Voyer, who seized every opportunity to appear on deck and chat with her lieutenant.

He was twenty years old and his name was Jean Dauvergne. His father had a business in Quebec, and this was the young man's last crossing as a ship's lieutenant. He was to settle down in New France and take charge of his father's affairs.

With the bemused indulgence of a maiden aunt, Jeanne encouraged these clandestine encounters. She stood guard near the rigging where Marie and Jean would discreetly sit, quietly exchanging the thousand nothings that make up lovers' conversation.

When someone approached, Jeanne would hum a tune, and like a guilty party, the young couple would leap to their feet. Marie would turn to Jeanne, eyes shining, stammering foolish things in a dreamy voice. Meanwhile, the lieutenant would busy himself checking the rigging or would gaze intently at a wave that was exactly like all the others.

Few things escaped Sister Bourgeoys, but if she did discover their secret, she had the discretion not to intervene.

By a stroke of luck both unfortunate and too good to be true, the other king's daughters fell victim to seasickness and didn't leave their dark, poorly ventilated cabins.

The six novices were preparing for their apostolate with seclusion and prayer. They appeared for mass that was celebrated on deck by a travelling priest when weather permitted. Otherwise, they were hardly to be seen.

One day, the look-out reported four sails in the distance. Rumours travel fast in the enclosed world of a ship. Soon all the passengers knew they were English vessels. Because of the state of war between France and England, it was feared these enemies would attempt to pursue and capture them.

The captain thought it his duty to assemble the passengers and announce this eventuality to them. Indignant protests, tears and shouts ensued.

"What will become of us?" asked the worried girls.

Remaining very calm, Sister Bourgeoys said in a loud, lively voice, "If those people capture us, well, then, we'll go to England or Holland and find God there as we would anywhere else."

Her witty reply reassured the less courageous among the group, and the captain was very glad to have this strong woman on board.

The ships disappeared on the horizon, and the voyage continued with no more of these alarms.

Jeanne, always ready to scrap, had hoped to witness a naval combat. She didn't realize she would have certainly been confined below deck where she would have seen nothing at all. She was almost disappointed to see the danger disappear.

But a different and even more formidable danger took its place.

A mysterious fever struck down five sailors. On an ocean voyage, the threat of an epidemic was to be feared more than the worst tempest. The captain, who knew of Marguerite Bourgeoys's reputation and devotion, relied on her competence. During each of her crossings, the seasoned traveller had rendered innumerable services.

She asked that all the sick be grouped together in the same place. Then she went to see them. Realizing she alone would not be equal to the task, she called the energetic, courageous Jeanne to her side.

The two women spent several days and nights caring for the unfortunate men, wiping the sweat from their feverish brows, making them swallow teas and concoctions of medicinal herbs. Sister Bourgeoys always carried ample supplies of them with her.

After five days of exhausting efforts, the sick men recovered and were declared out of danger—except for one: François Legrand.

The young seventeen-year-old Norman was growing weaker by the hour, and soon he lapsed into a fatal coma. Nothing more could be done for him, and Sister Bourgeoys, worn out by her long vigils, was forced to take some rest. Jeanne had just slept for a few hours, and she replaced her at the dying boy's bedside.

Crouched on a stool by the narrow bunk, the helpless girl watched his gaunt face and listened to his gasping breath. She asked that a lantern be lit in the dark cubbyhole, for she felt herself transported back to that night long ago when her grandfather lay on his deathbed.

Perhaps it was he in the end who hadn't wanted to meet his death in darkness? François must be reassured in the same way, Jeanne reasoned.

As she was putting a damp towel on his feverish fore-head, the boy opened his eyes. For the first time in two days, he regained consciousness. With a claw-like hand, he grasped his nurse's fingers.

"Miss, I'm going to die. I'm afraid of dying all alone at sea. I'm afraid."

"You're not alone, François. I'm right beside you. I won't leave you."

Gently she led him to recite his act of contrition. The priest had given him last rites a few hours earlier.

Jeanne spoke of the Virgin and God's goodness, as she knew Sister Bourgeoys would have. But the boy didn't let go of her hand, and she could see the terror in his dark eyes.

Then, in a gentle, even voice, Jeanne Chatel told the little sailor from Normandy who didn't want to die the beautiful version of death that her grandfather had handed down to her.

"You'll go to a big garden of dreams where you'll meet all the people you've ever loved in your life. Even your dogs. Did you ever have a dog, François?"

"Yes. When I was a little boy. A big dog with curly hair who used to sleep with me. His name was Miraud."

"Well, then, François, Miraud is waiting for you and he'll welcome you with a wag of his tail. You'll do everything you liked to do on earth."

"Will I play my flute?"

Like a trusting child—as Jeanne once had been—François became a willing partner in the game they were playing.

Jeanne was not sure whether Marguerite Bourgeoys or

the priest would approve of her own private version of paradise, but if God was good as she believed he was, he wouldn't disappoint a simple, naive sailor. For a long time they plotted in low tones.

Reassured, the dying boy shut his eyes, and a smile played at his pale lips. He was preparing his own paradise. Jeanne prayed beside him, asking her grandfather to take in this poor abandoned child.

"Miss," François breathed, "look in my trunk. I want to give you a present."

"That's not necessary," Jeanne protested, though she was deeply moved. But seeing her patient grow restless, she opened the old trunk that had been pulled next to the bed.

"There at the bottom, in my clean shirt. The Spanish shawl...it's for you. I bought it in port to give to a girl back home, the one I would have married."

"If you want to tell me her name, I'll send it to her for you."

François smiled sadly. "She has no name. I haven't chosen her yet. Take it. I'll look down upon you from paradise and I'll think how beautiful you are."

He fell silent, exhausted, and Jeanne, with her instinctive knowledge of what gives pleasure to others, draped the magnificent red and green flowered shawl over her grey dress. The long silky fringe glistened in the lamplight, and her grey eyes, wet with tears, were soft and tender. François gazed at her for a long time.

Suddenly he squeezed her hand and in a calm voice said, "Goodnight, miss. I'm going now."

His curly head fell back. Jeanne gently pulled up the sheet to cover his relaxed, peaceful face. "Bon voyage,

François. Say hello to my grandfather. And wait for me there, both of you," she murmured softly.

The next day, before the assembled crew and passengers, the slender body, sewn into a large sail, was cast into the sea. Instead of her usual coif, Jeanne Chatel was wrapped in a gaudy shawl whose iridescent colours stood out from the group's dark clothing. Disapproving eyes turned towards her. But Marguerite Bourgeoys, who had been entrusted with the story, had given her approval with the open-mindedness that put her far ahead of her time.

Under the cold sun of the Atlantic, on that little vessel that was but a tiny dot on the grey ocean, all the lights seemed to gather on the Spanish shawl. Jeanne clasped the gold medal that hung around her neck. She was sure that François Legrand and Honoré Chatel were watching her with pleasure from their paradise. She felt the warmth of their presence all around her; of all the passengers, she alone watched with dry eyes as the waves closed over the corpse of the seventeen-year-old boy.

A few days later, when a rope gave way, pitching two sailors from the main mast, it seemed quite natural to call on Marguerite Bourgeoys and her appointed assistant. With the help of three strong men who held down the injured, the nun reset the broken bones and sewed up the wounds. Pale with compassion, Jeanne helped as best she knew how.

Fighting nausea as she held the unfortunate sailors' heads, she slipped a piece of wood between their clenched teeth in order to muffle their cries of pain.

When the brutal surgery was over and the sailors were finally unconscious and as comfortable as possible, Jeanne ran to the rail of the ship. At last she could succumb to her nausea and sink to her knees. Sister Bourgeoys came to her side and gently offered her a damp cloth to wipe her sweaty face.

"I'm sorry for this weakness," murmured Jeanne, ashamed.

"On the contrary, my child. You were admirable when you were needed. This is the perfectly human reaction of a sensitive person. Already I can foresee the generous contribution you'll make to our colony. It's souls like yours that we need the most."

"I'm not very adept at prayer," admitted Jeanne frankly.

"You're a good girl. You'll help others. That will be your way of praying. Some people's devotion is more useful than others'. You will be one of those."

Sister Bourgeoys retired, leaving Jeanne to contemplate the surging waves and low sky.

Jeanne was happy that someone had confidence in her at last. If it wasn't for her enthusiasm and natural light-heartedness, she would have given in to frustration long ago. With the exception of Sister Berthelet, the good nuns of the congregation had never been entirely satisfied with her efforts. All her life, her character had been unfavourably compared to Marie's gentleness, Anne's piety, Geneviève's industriousness and the modesty of all the others.

Fortunately, ten years of security with her grandfather had given her a store of optimism and a reserve of warmth that had sustained her in the dark hours when the convent routine threatened to crush her spirit.

6

ONE day, the look-out sighted land at last. The travellers were a little disappointed to spot only a thin dark line on the horizon, but soon the ship sailed past the high rocky cliffs of Newfoundland. Then the coast of Nova Scotia paraded before their eyes.

The St. Lawrence narrowed but still appeared gigantic compared to the watercourses of France. Sometimes they rounded a green island set like an emerald in the steel-grey ribbon of the river. The wind brought them the invigorating scent of the pines that bordered the shores and came down right to the banks.

One morning as the passengers on deck were admiring the rocks jutting over the Saguenay River, Sister Bourgeoys took Jeanne to the narrow cabin she shared with five of the novices. With a laugh, the seasoned traveller told her companions that the dark little cubby-hole represented a luxury for her. Indeed, she had already made the crossing on deck, sleeping in the open on the ropes, in the days when she had been too poor to afford a bed on board.

"Jeanne," said Sister Bourgeoys, "I've prepared this bag for you. It will help you help others. I can see in you a great need for devotion; that will be your greatest asset in your new life."

She handed Jeanne a heavy, square leather sack, fitted with a strap so it could be carried over the shoulder.

"I've filled this bag with medicines and curative herbs. I collected ample supplies before I left France," the nun went on.

Setting the sack on the narrow bench that served as a bed, she opened it and showed her charge an assortment of smaller sacks, glass bottles and flasks, all carefully labelled. A small book full of notes came along with it.

"Here you will find the description of every remedy, the illnesses they're used for, doses and the effects to expect. I know you are diligent enough to study it and benefit from it. And you must not neglect the knowledge of the many wise people you will meet.

"Always be on the alert for new curative plants. New France has many that the Indians or settlers will show you. The Indians possess the secrets of some very efficient cures."

Marguerite Bourgeoys closed the sack and added a little slyly, "And neither should you forget the very positive moral effect of a harmless potion when the true nature of the illness escapes you. I have often cured dizziness with sugared warm water. And mothers sleep better when they have a medicine to give their children at regular intervals. It reassures them and doubles their courage."

Jeanne listened attentively, her grey eyes intently watching the wrinkled face of her benefactress. She considered herself a soldier being entrusted with a mission.

"You will not have put your confidence in me in vain, sister," the orphan passionately declared. "I've already learned much during this crossing, and before we set foot in Quebec, I will know this notebook by heart."

Jeanne's zeal confirmed Marguerite Bourgeoys's opinion. The old nun was a good judge of women of action and she had discovered one of that breed in this difficult student in whom Mother de Chablais couldn't find one good quality.

Jeanne carried the heavy sack to her cabin, took out the notebook and emptied the medicines onto the straw mattress. She plunged into the study of this new science, and every free moment found her murmuring,

"Marseilles vinegar for the plague.

Melissa cordial for migraine.

Poppy for bronchitis.

Hawthorn for the heart.

Paregoric for relief of pain."

If it was up to Jeanne Chatel, the colony would be bursting with perpetual health and would soon contain only alert hundred-year-olds and bouncing babies.

7

QUEBEC, *August, 1672*

On a beautiful evening in the month of August, the sailing ship passed Ile d'Orléans and approached the fortified city of Quebec, perched on the heights of its gigantic cliff.

The royal flag was flapping in the wind above the log fortifications of Chateau Saint-Louis, which towered over the rock. Jeanne looked up proudly at that symbol of the courage and tenacity of her compatriots.

Several wooden houses nestled in the shadow of Cap Diamant. Canoes and small boats of all types were beached on the shore. In the distance, a steep road scaled the cliff, leading to the upper part of the town.

If the departure from Le Havre had seemed picturesque to Jeanne, the arrival in Quebec left her speechless. Besides the governor's delegation presenting arms with a flourish of trumpets, she saw a crowd of citizens on the wharf attracted by this much anticipated event: the arrival of a ship. The coureurs de bois with their strange fringed shirts and their fur caps never parted with their guns. To her the Indians seemed peaceful, even somewhat dazed, and she couldn't figure out why people spoke of them with such terror. At the time she did not know those Indians had been transformed by living with the whites; they had nothing in common with their brothers, the fierce kings of the forest.

The passengers, gathered on deck with their trunks and suitcases, silently studied the grand scenery spread before them. The less courageous felt overwhelmed by that immense rock, that gigantic river, those endless forests they had been sailing by for days. How distant were the peaceful contours and gentle colours of the French countryside!

Leaning against the rail between Jeanne and her lieutenant, Marie looked around with frightened eyes.

"Everything seems so big, so threatening," she shivered.

"No, it's all magnificent," contradicted Jeanne enthusiastically. "The air smells of pine. You can see that the country is brand-new."

With a great uproar of shouting and noise, the gangplank finally linked the ship with solid ground.

Monsieur de Frontenac, the governor who had just taken office, came forward, hat in hand. Sister Bourgeoys was the first to cross the narrow wooden plank. The Quebeckers cheered her, knowing that each of her numerous voyages contributed to the colony's well-being.

At a signal from the captain, the king's daughters, led by Jeanne, set foot on the soil of New France. Many of them were disappointed that the rolling and pitching sensation of the ship didn't disappear, but persisted for several hours.

From a distance, the awed Quebeckers inspected these girls daring enough to land in a wild country with no protection other than that offered by a potential husband. The married men looked at what they had missed, and the bachelors took inventory of the possibilities.

The girls, embarrassed by all those covetous glances, blushed and lowered their eyes. Only Jeanne, filled with wonder and fascination, looked at everything around her and answered the murmured words of welcome with an open smile.

The local women surrounded them, full of questions about the price of food in France and about fashions in Paris. The six novices and the king's daughters, fresh from the convent, were unable to answer them, and the curious women swooped down on other better-informed passengers.

Sister Bourgeoys reassembled her little troupe and preceded them through the narrow streets of the Lower Town.

Jeanne lingered behind, stopping to examine an Indian woman carrying her baby strapped to her back in a strange leather and wood cocoon.

"How practical," she marvelled. "That leaves your hands free to work. You have a beautiful baby," she assured the woman, who stared back at her impassively. But a flash of maternal pride lit her dark eyes.

Jeanne picked up her skirts and dashed off after the dainty group of king's daughters. Her white-stockinged legs agilely cleaved the air. Marie was absolutely scandalized.

"You're not thinking, Jeanne, running through the streets like an urchin. What would Mother de Chablais say? A lady doesn't do that."

"That's right," the thoughtless girl humbly admitted. "I'm not a lady, far from it."

Nonetheless, she wasn't about to hang her head. The little town answered the description she had read in *Real and Natural History*, written in 1663 by Pierre Boucher. Noticing Jeanne's interest in her future homeland, Marguerite Bourgeoys had given her this book before she left Troyes. Better educated and brighter than her companions, Jeanne Chatel had showered her protectress with countless questions. This modest work written by the governor of Trois-Rivières had only partly satisfied her curiosity. She knew entire passages of it by heart.

"Quebec is situated on the shore of the mighty St. Lawrence River, which at that spot is barely a league wide and flows between two heights. This fortress, the churches and monasteries and finest houses are built on top; other houses and stores are built at the foot of the hill, on the shore of the great river, to service the ships that stop there..."

Sister Bourgeoys took her girls to Widow Myrand's little house. The widow ran an inn in the Lower Town, and they would be staying there for the few days it took to prepare for the departure to Ville-Marie. They had to reserve the flat-bottomed boats and oarsmen who would row them up the current on the exhausting seven- or eight-day voyage.

Widow Myrand, surly and not at all pleasant, showed her guests to rooms as small and overcrowded as those on the ship they had just left. No one complained. A spirit of self-denial was essential baggage for those who came to colonize the new world.

Robust young men put the eleven girls' trunks in the common room. They took their leave after sidelong glances and awkward salutations, pressing to their hearts the wool caps they wore even in summer. Jeanne examined them immodestly and mentally rejected them, one after the other. Not one of them met her excessive demands. Unknowingly, the sentimental girl was searching for Thierry de Villebrand in all the suitors' faces. That was the best way to be disappointed, she knew, but she couldn't help it.

Despite the late hour, Sister Bourgeoys left her charges after cautioning them to be careful. They were not to go out. The Indians might be on the prowl. She didn't say so, but the settlers and soldiers presented a much more tangible danger to these young turtle doves who were such a rare commodity in New France.

The nun climbed the steep slope of Côte de la Montagne to pay her respects to the bishop's delegate. Monseigneur de Laval, her old adversary with whom she had had difficult conflicts in the past, was currently in France. The authoritarian prelate would have been very happy to see this refractory nun subject to the rules of a cloister, like that of the Ursulines. Sister Bourgeoys refused, maintaining that her missionary work had to be done outside the cloister, and that by remaining secular and free to come and go as she pleased, she was better able to help the colony.

The traveller would also visit the Ursulines where she would spend the night. Unfortunately, her good friend, Mother Marie de l'Incarnation, who had always been happy to welcome her, had died the previous April.

Marguerite Bourgeoys's latest absence had lasted two years. Many things had changed during that time. Intendant Talon and Monsieur de Courcelle, the governor, had been recalled to France. Monsieur de Frontenac, who was said to be energetic and courageous, was now occupying the Chateau Saint-Louis.

The founder of the congregation painstakingly climbed the steep slope. She, too, was happy to be on solid ground once again, and was pleased she had brought back new recruits for this country she loved so much.

8

GRUMBLING, Widow Myrand served a frugal meal that seemed sumptuous after the salted meat, dried biscuits and rancid water that had been the girls' menu on board ship.

Jeanne, overexcited by the liveliness and noise of the town, still unaccustomed to feeling solid ground beneath her feet, asked for and received permission to sit on the doorstep with Marie. The two of them chatted quietly in the semi-darkness, though Marie dominated the conversation, inexhaustible when it came to her lieutenant's endless good qualities. The little grey mouse from the dormitory had been transfigured.

"You know, Jeanne, we're going to get married and Jean is going to settle here in Quebec where his father has a business."

"And what will your fiancé, Monsieur Simon de Rouville, say?"

Marie was in love. All obstacles were pushed aside. "Oh, he'll understand and marry another of the king's daughters. You, for example."

"Thank you so much. At least leave me the privilege of choosing."

That old widower in search of a housekeeper wasn't even worth mentioning.

Footsteps neared the house. "That's Jean!" exclaimed Marie, who had been watching for him.

The young man stepped forward with a firm tread and bowed to the two friends. Relieved of his duties on board ship for the evening, he had gone to greet his parents in Cap Diamant. Then he had come down as soon as possible to be with his beloved. They had little time to plan and an entire happy life to prepare for.

Jeanne discreetly moved a few steps away, leaving the young couple to speak their hearts' desire. She felt elderly and protective. All her sisterly love went out to that trusting girl and sincere young man. She wished them happiness.

Leaning against the side of the small house, a few steps from the street that was deserted at that hour, Jeanne listened to the silence. It amazed her after the constant noise that had assailed her ears on board ship. The scent of earth and pine mingled with that of the few tenacious flowers that bordered Madame Myrand's little garden.

Suddenly an apparition surged out of the night. A grimacing face, crossed by a scar and crowned by two feathers, materialized soundlessly before her, blocking her retreat. Sister Bourgeoys was right. The Indians were as bold as could be. The terrifying stories with which the sailors enjoyed regaling the girls—despite Sister Bourgeoys's vigilance—came back to Jeanne. In a flash she thought, If I scream, Jean and Marie will come to my aid and be killed. She did not cry out, but slowly began walking, step by step, into the night. She surrendered all hope of rescue, but at least she diverted the danger from those she loved.

Without a word, without a sound, the Indian followed

her, looming up between her and the house. He put his hand out. Was he holding a knife? Jeanne dared to venture a look...and was surprised to see that it was a piece of paper. And a closer look showed that his sinister face expressed more perplexity than hatred, and that his grimace was a smile.

Jeanne snatched the note from his outstretched hand and stepped past the Indian. Unable to utter a sound, she hurried towards the inn and brushed unceremoniously past Marie and Jean who had hardly noticed her. She collapsed into the low chair in front of the candle where Widow Myrand was dozing in her rocking chair. Accustomed to the early hours on board ship, Sister Bourgeoys's charges were saying their prayers or already asleep in the loft.

Jeanne, still quite pale, leaned towards the flickering light and began deciphering Marguerite Bourgeoys's hand-writing. She knew it well from having helped her make up shopping lists in Rouen. The letter was addressed to Widow Myrand. Jeanne gave it to that good woman who, rather than admit she didn't know how to read, claimed her eyesight was bad and declared she was all ears.

Jeanne read the words swimming there before her eyes, doing her best to conceal the trembling of her voice.

Dear Madame:
This letter is to inform Mademoiselle Marie du Voyer of an urgent situation. Her fiancé, Monsieur de Rouville, needs her in Ville-Marie immediately, due to the lateness of the season. A group of travellers, accompanied by two Sulpician priests and two women, will leave tomorrow at dawn by canoe, and Mademoiselle du Voyer is granted per-

mission to accompany them. In Ville-Marie, she will take up residence at the Bon-Secours School, where all arrangements have been made for her marriage to Monsieur de Rouville. He most definitely wishes to reach his lands before winter sets in. Wishing Mademoiselle du Voyer all possible happiness in her saintly destiny, I place her under the protection of Notre Dame du Bon-Secours.

The usual greetings and the founder's signature followed.

Jeanne was shattered. Just then the door opened and Marie came in, eyes shining. To preserve the spell she was under, she went past her friend without a word. Wishing her good night with a little wave of her hand, she climbed the steep stairway that led to the attic where the girls slept. With a lover's selfishness, she fell asleep to dream of her happiness, not realizing it had just collapsed.

Jeanne went to the doorway and saw the motionless form of the Indian waiting by the steps. As before when she believed her friends were in danger, just as instinctively, just as rapidly, her resolution took shape. She turned to Widow Myrand who, candle in hand, was hoping that all her excited boarders would finally solve their problems and let her go to bed.

"Madame Myrand, if you can help me pull my trunk over near the door, this Indian will help me take it out. And if you would leave me the candle and give me something to write with, you can go to bed and I won't wake you when I leave at dawn."

"Oh?" said the widow, not very interested. "So you're Mademoiselle du Voyer?"

"Yes, I am," said Jeanne calmly. "And my fiancé is waiting for me in Ville-Marie."

9

ON the banks of the St. Lawrence, September, 1672

Dear Marie,

I'm writing flat on my stomach on the soaking wet ground. I'm using the notebook Sister Bourgeoys gave me on board ship for the first time to record my spiritual thoughts. I'm supposed to be dry under a canvas sheet that a Sulpician father and one of the voyageurs gallantly stretched from some poles and baptized a shelter. The rain drips from the leaves and everything I touch, eat or breathe is wet. The Indians have managed to light a fire that is smoking between two rocks, and their skin glistens with a red glow. They gave me some kind of food called pemmican that's both greasy and hard. The women mentioned in Mademoiselle Bourgeoys's letter are two Hurons as silent as their men.

The Indians, the voyageurs and the two Sulpician fathers have been paddling for two days, bent under the rain, following the river bank. After Cap Rouge, not a single settlement, except for two isolated farms and the blackened ruins of a third.

They call me Mademoiselle du Voyer and I answer as if it had always been my name. What will Monsieur Simon de Rouville say when he discovers the hoax? If ever you read these words, it will be because everything has worked out. You will find happiness with your Jean and Monsieur de Rouville will either have accepted or rejected me. I came here as a king's daughter to marry a settler in New France, and in my heart, deep down in my heart, I knew my beautiful dreams of a proud military man, of a gallant lord or a rich farmer were just that—dreams.

At least if your own dream becomes reality, then one of us will have succeeded. Here's my lovely notebook all wet and limp, and the writing almost illegible. It doesn't matter. I'm not writing to be read, but to feel less alone.

At another campfire...

The journey continues between two deserted shores. This river is so wide we often lose sight of the other side. Constantly I think of how disappointed Monsieur de Rouville will be when, instead of the pretty cousin he's been waiting for, he sees an orphan with her hair pulled back in braids, a pale face and colourless eyes. Even as a governess, am I what he would wish for? And suddenly I realize his choice will involve my whole life, and I'm very afraid, much more than of the Iroquois. Tomorrow we arrive. If the rain stops, perhaps my hair will dry.

10

VILLE-MARIE, *September 7, 1672*

Dear Marie,
Your fiancé saw me and I don't know yet how to inter-pret his reaction. Here's what happened. The trip lasted five days, which is very fast, so they told me with great satisfac-tion.

The canoe travelled past an island called Sault Normand, then turned abruptly and headed towards the shore. Near the mouth of a little river, I spotted the stock-ade of a fort. On the left, among the scruffy trees, a few cul-tivated fields surrounded a chapel and a couple of stone buildings that looked like barns to me; a Sulpician father proudly pointed them out as Mademoiselle Mance's hospital and Sister Bourgeoys's Bon-Secours School. Here and there were a few houses, and in the distance was the silhouette of a rounded mountain with a cross on top: Mount Royal.

When the canoe was about a hundred feet from the bank, all the voyageurs let out loud shouts and waved their paddles. When they heard the noise, the soldiers fired their muskets into the air, the chapel bells began to ring and peo-ple—men, women and children—came out of the houses and the woods and rushed down the gentle slope to meet us.

The voyageurs and Indians beached the canoes and jumped into the water, some of them up to their waists, in spite of the cold. I was ordered to remain seated, and they all lifted the heavy boat and placed it high and dry on the sand. I really did feel like the king's daughter. One of the voyageurs shouted, "Rouville, here's your fiancée!"

From among the villagers waiting on the side, I searched out the pot-bellied old man who would correspond to the image I had of your future husband, ever since I first read his letter.

A tall slim man came forward, dressed in a coureur de bois fringed shirt. He leaned on his long rifle and gave me a long, silent look. The setting sun kept me from seeing his face but it illuminated mine, which must have already been blushing. He didn't seem like a very gallant fiancé to me. Perhaps he was disappointed. I had just had time to plunk a cap—probably the wrong way round—on my tousled hair. Camp life doesn't lend itself to stylishness.

Nevertheless, a friendly phrase or a word of welcome never costs you anything. Monsieur de Rouville said brusquely, "I will see you this evening at Bon-Secours." And he turned on his heels and went off to talk to one of Hurons who accompanied us. He spoke with authority, and the others seemed to fear him.

Fortunately the women made a big fuss over me, questioning me, wanting news of Quebec and France. They inquired after people in the colony and the prices in Europe. Since I was poorly informed about both, I mustn't have made much of an impression. They took me and my trunk to the school which, as I had guessed, was an old barn. They left me in the hands of a Mademoiselle Catherine Crolo *and other assistants of Sister Bourgeoys.*

After a supper that seemed like a banquet, since it featured vegetables and fresh fruit after the rations of the canoe trip and the crossing, I decked myself out in my best finery. Despite all my efforts, the only mirror I found in the school still showed me the same pale face, the same rings around my grey eyes. Fatigue made me look ashen, and I was exhausted and nervous. Tenderly I thought of you and Jean, and your happiness gave me courage.

When Monsieur de Rouville appeared soon after the meal, he still had his precious firearm. From up close, I found his tanned face rather pleasing. He has regular features, pale, piercing eyes and black hair that he wears short. He seemed very ill at ease and I can't blame him, since Mademoiselle Crolo took her role as chaperon seriously and didn't leave us alone for a minute. We sat side by side on the same bench, avoiding looking at each other.

As his first words, "our" fiancé announced, "If it's convenient for you, Mademoiselle du Voyer, since we have to leave for my estate before winter, Father Lefebvre, father superior of the seminary, will solemnize our marriage on Friday." Estate? What estate?

I felt as though I had to stop a runaway horse. I didn't know where to begin my protests and explanations. I started with the most urgent.

"I am not Mademoiselle du Voyer."

And in one fell swoop, I explained your story as clearly as I could. His reaction was unexpected.

"But just the same you're a king's daughter, aren't you? You're ready to get married on Friday? I must go right away and inform Father Lefebvre of the change of name."

He executed a quick bow and, without another word, he fled as if a dragon were chasing him.

I was wavering between anger and tears when he burst into the room again. "I didn't hear your real name. What is it?"

I flung it at him and added spitefully, "You should also know I'm older than you think."

He frowned. He was expecting a child of fifteen. In his harsh voice he asked, "Oh? And how old are you then, mademoiselle?"

I faced him with dignity. "I am eighteen, nearly nineteen."

He smiled ironically and said in a mocking voice, "That's a respectable age indeed. Almost an old maid."

Mademoiselle Crolo coughed discreetly. I was furious. Didn't he see how distressing and false my situation was, and couldn't he help me instead of mocking me in front of our chaperon? I'm sure that faced with your beauty and gentleness, he would have reacted quite differently.

And that's how it is that on Friday I will marry a perfect stranger and go and live in an unknown land with the approval of the father superior and the blessing of the whole colony. I hope you will be happy, Marie. I have the feeling I'm paying for your happiness with mine.

11

VILLE-MARIE, *September 7, 1672*

Dear Marie,

I'm finishing this notebook with the pitiable account of my wedding. I will leave it in the hands of Mademoiselle Crolo, and in a year, when we return to Ville-Marie to sell the furs my husband will have trapped during the winter, I will add an epilogue to it. If it is a happy ending, you will receive this notebook by messenger; if it is unhappy, I will burn it and you will think your friend has disappeared into the savage wilderness. You will mourn her a little as you cradle your blond children in your arms.

For a wedding present my fiancé solemnly handed me...a musket. He made me swear never to part with it. All the men admired it and I was wondering what Mother de Chablais and our companions in the congregation would say about such a present.

The marriage ceremony was simple and quick, as everything is in New France. The groom and the guests left their weapons at the chapel door and picked them up again as they left. They fear the Iroquois even in the town. The groom wore a wool suit and seemed very uncomfortable in his hard shoes.

At the last minute a substitution had to be made because, so they said, the man who was to act as my husband's witness hadn't returned on time from an expedition to Huronia. Instead of Captain de Preux, Simon de Rouville's school friend and comrade-in-arms, a lieutenant whose name I forget stood up with the groom. Since I knew neither of the two officers in question, I wasn't the least concerned.

I held the wildflowers a woman had slipped into my hands in place of a bridal bouquet; I thought I was living a dream.

After Father Lefebvre asked me the traditional question twice, and my lord gave me an imperious poke with his elbow to call me to order, I murmured yes in a tiny voice. He wasn't so hesitant. His yes resounded through the church and made me cold all over. It seemed to say, "Obviously I want to marry her; that's why I'm here. Let's get all this nonsense over with and let's get going. I have more urgent things to attend to."

It was done. We were husband and wife and I didn't even know his age or just what colour his eyes were.

Everybody took my change of name very naturally. From du Voyer, there I was Chatel and the next moment Madame de Rouville. People here don't care about details. Life is too short and too intense.

On the chapel steps, as I was being congratulated, three people told me how much I resembled Aimée, Monsieur de Rouville's first wife. Now I understand why he accepted me so quickly. This resemblance gives him the illusion of taking up his life at the point where it was broken. He was on a hunting trip when the Iroquois burned down his house and killed his wife and son. The Huron servant fled into the forest with the two other children. He blamed himself for not having defended his wife well enough, but by a miracle she has been returned to him thanks to an unfortunate resemblance. Monsieur de Rouville is going to have the extraordinary opportunity to literally reconstruct his life.

That explains the gift of the musket and also your friend's discouragement. It wasn't good enough being a second-hand fiancée; now here I am a replacement wife. We are leaving immediately by canoe for the southern part of the region where my husband has a house, a field and his hunting grounds. On the way we will pick up his two children who are being kept by a family. An old Huron woman who was his first wife's servant will accompany us. And we will spend the winter (that they say is long and cold) in some far-off part of the forest.

That all happened this morning. And here I am now back with the congregation nuns, spending the afternoon while my husband makes the final preparations for our departure at dawn tomorrow. Everyone seems to have dispersed immediately after the ceremony, since no one can afford to lose a day's work, even to attend a wedding supper.

I found myself back at Bon-Secours with orders to pack up my trunk and keep only what would be useful on the journey tomorrow. At the last minute my lord and master said over his shoulder, "You may also keep some finery, since there will be a dance in our honour tonight. I'll come get you at eight o'clock."

Isn't that gallant? Am I not spoiled?

I'm letting myself be carried along by events, indifferent to everything, too much out of my element to have any reac-

tions, too uninformed to nourish hope. What will this winter be like, my first one in New France, with this silent lord, this taciturn Huron woman and the children of Aimée whose place I'm taking? You will know the answer in a year's time. Adieu, Marie. May God keep us.

12

"THERE will be a dance in our honour." Jeanne had a great number of questions about that subject, but Mademoiselle Crolo lived withdrawn from society, and she was unable to enlighten her.

Jeanne bent over her trunk and searched in vain for some "finery." All her dresses were grey, and Mother de Chablais's idea of stylishness was a white coif and matching starched collar.

Jeanne Chatel had never been one to rack her brains over an unsolvable problem. She took the Spanish shawl and draped it over her shoulders, abandoning the white scarf that was proper attire for any modest woman. She made sure her white cap hid her hair completely. Then she sat down by the hearth to wait for her husband.

We're finishing at the beginning, she thought bitterly. He's taking me to the ball after he married me, and he married me before he knew me.

Dismayed, the nun objected to the king's daughter's style of dress. "A modest girl doesn't wear garish colours like that."

"Mother Crolo, isn't it my duty to please my husband?"

"You will please him with your virtues."

Jeanne laughed sarcastically. "Then he'll have to be content with very little."

Just then a military officer presented himself at the school door and greeted her courteously.

"Madame, I am Lieutenant Pierre de Touron. I acted as witness to your marriage. Monsieur de Rouville asked me to escort you to the dance, for he has been delayed by urgent business. He will join us later at the governor's house. It's a great honour for me."

"What!" Jeanne exclaimed, horrified. "Is the ball taking place at the governor's house? That's terrible. I have neither the clothes nor the manners for such a fête. I can't go."

"On the contrary, madame," protested the gallant soldier, looking approvingly at her well-made figure. The shawl she had wrapped herself in lent some colour to her pale face. "You will be the queen of the ball—and not only because you'll be the heroine."

Never had an orphan heard such a beautiful speech. Tongue-tied for once, she let the young man help her on with her big grey cape, the coat worn by novices and king's daughters alike. Putting her hand on her escort's arm—as if she had been used to doing that all her life—Madame de Rouville, head high, stepped out with the handsome officer. That's the sort of husband she needed: eager, eloquent and obviously overflowing with admiration. They went briskly down the road that led to the fort, and Jeanne noticed two armed soldiers escorting them. In Ville-Marie, you couldn't even go to a ball without running the risk of meeting danger.

As Marguerite Bourgeoys's ward walked along in her uncomfortably new leather shoes, she soon had much more down-to-earth worries. She did not know how to dance and had never in her life attended a social gathering. A good ten times she was tempted to reverse her steps and run back to the refuge offered by the Bon-Secours School, but pride prevented her. She was going to show that Monsieur de Rouville, who was too overworked to pay any attention to his wife on their wedding day! She'd show him that Jeanne Chatel could manage very well by herself!

The sentinels saluted the couples as they came into the fort enclosure one after another. Pine torches and lanterns lit up the warm night. Near the wall, Monsieur François-Marie Perrot, the governor, haughty and cantankerous, and his scarcely more likeable wife were welcoming their guests. The lieutenant and Jeanne traded deep bows with them.

Already couples were gaily dancing under the stars in the centre of the regiment's parade ground. An orchestra composed of three musicians was playing lively melodies. Under a tree, large pots of spruce beer awaited the thirsty guests. Farther along, brandy was served.

Jeanne was relieved. She had feared a big court ball with all the pomp and traditional ceremony. This boisterous gaiety reassured her a little.

"Here comes the bride!" shouted the guests, breaking off the saraband. Joyful exclamations greeted this announcement.

"The bride will open the ball," proclaimed a noisy, strapping fellow.

A circle immediately formed around the new arrivals. The musicians tackled a wild rhythm, and the lieutenant, throwing Jeanne's cape onto a wooden bench, held out his hands to her.

"I don't know how to dance," Jeanne admitted, embarrassed.

"Just follow me," Pierre de Touron reassured her. "Do what I do and nobody will notice a thing. They're far too busy admiring and envying you."

The lieutenant took hold of his partner and led her, in step, across the grounds. Then, grasping her firmly around the waist with both hands, he turned her faster and faster. Jeanne was supple and agile and had a good sense of rhythm. She fell into step almost before she knew it.

Little by little, other couples began dancing. Light on her feet, a little out of breath, the new bride fairly flew in her partner's strong arms. Her unusual timidness gave way to the pure joy of life; her bursts of laughter were infectious. She changed partners every other minute and jauntily went from arm to arm. Lieutenant de Touron returned for more than his share, and his saucy compliments made the colour rise in the king's daughter's cheeks.

Her grey eyes sparkled with pleasure. She threw back her head and her brown locks escaped from the modest white cap; recovering their natural shape, they curled into wild ringlets. Her grey skirt swirled, revealing fine ankles wrapped in white trousseau stockings. Jeanne never suspected it, since everyone had always tried to make a modest girl of her, but she could be very pretty when she was full of life—as she was tonight.

That is what the amazed Monsieur de Rouville realized when he arrived at the party, stern and frowning, his gun slung over his shoulder.

That gaudy shawl, that wild hair, that abandon on the dance floor—was all this quite fitting for the wife of a worthy and respected lord? And all those sweaty noisy men fighting for the honour of spinning his wife in their arms!

68

The stormy look on his face fell like a cold shower on the gathering.

The musicians fell silent, the dancers came to rest. But nothing discouraged the sociable fellow who exclaimed, "Here comes the groom. And it's none too soon. Simon, you must dance with your wife!"

Shouts of approval rang out. The groom had to agree. He carefully leaned his musket against a tree and approached Jeanne, standing motionless, still out of breath, next to her last and most persistent partner, Lieutenant de Touron.

With cutting irony, Rouville said to his friend, "I'm relieving you of your duties. They don't seem to have been too demanding."

"You have given me more difficult missions in the past," countered the soldier without losing face.

He turned to Jeanne and said gravely, "Madame, it is with much regret that I return you to your husband. Don't forget that from this evening onward, I am your devoted servant for life."

Jeanne, unaccustomed to these extravagant phrases, and very embarrassed at such boldness in front of her stern husband, did not know how to reply. Pierre bowed with the ease of a nobleman at the court of Versailles and kissed his partner's hand, which had suddenly grown icy. Dazzled, Jeanne stared at her hand in amazement; she had forgotten to put it down again. It was like a storybook. Jeanne Chatel, the orphan from the congregation nuns, the outlawed poacher's little girl, had just had her hand kissed by a handsome young gentleman.

A bantering voice drew her from her momentary paralysis.

"May I tear you away from your dreams, and would you permit me to take this consecrated hand and dance with me? Our friends desire it."

And indeed, the applause and shouts urged them into action. Monsieur de Rouville seemed to be well liked despite his cloudy countenance. The voices rang out, loud and bawdy.

"Come on, Simon. Show us the Iroquois step."

"Your wife dances well, Rouville. You're the only one who doesn't know it yet."

"Dance, old boy. You won't dance much this winter."

As the affectionate gibes fell like hail, the groom's face relaxed, and a smile revealed his dazzling white teeth.

So he knows how to smile, Jeanne thought bitterly. But only for other people.

Bending his tall frame, Simon asked gently, "Madame, do you have enough strength left to accompany me?"

Taken aback, she nodded without a word.

The music began again. Jeanne felt herself being carried off in an iron grip. Simon was holding her much too tightly; it was difficult to be light-footed in those conditions. Stiff and awkward now, she missed a step and stumbled. Inwardly she was fuming; this mocking, melancholy man was always catching her off guard.

The quadrille seemed endless to the poor girl. Simon made all the figures effortlessly, but he seemed preoccupied and it was obvious he was thinking about something else.

As soon as the music stopped, he pulled her along in his wake without asking her opinion. He threw the grey cape over her shoulders, picked up his musket and, after waving to the group, made his way to the door.

The governor made the appearance protocol demanded of him, then fled from those miserable settlers he despised to take refuge in his quarters. The dance became much more rollicking as a result of his departure.

Simon moved along with giant steps, forcing Jeanne to run to keep up with him. Did he think she was going to let herself be dragged along like a docile little dog on a leash? But that was what was happening, as she grumbled under her breath. Impatient, he executed a half turn in her direction and slowed his pace.

As soon as they were outside the wall of the fort and had gone past the sentries who saluted them, Simon gave a low whistle. Two figures immediately came from the shadows and followed in their footsteps. Did the brave Monsieur de Rouville himself feel the need for protection in the heart of Ville-Marie? What would he need on his isolated estate, then? An army ready to wage war?

An owl hooted in the distance, and another answered close by. Jeanne's poacher's heart skipped a beat. Maybe those owls had feathers, but they didn't have wings—that was for sure.

Simon stopped near a clump of trees. Carried by her momentum, Jeanne bumped into his large back that blocked the way.

The two men who had been following them suddenly seemed to vanish into the night. Branches parted noiselessly on either side of them. They were surrounded.

Jeanne's heart beat wildly. "Give me a knife," she whispered to Simon in a voice that brooked no refusal.

At least she might have a chance to defend herself. She cursed the coquetry that had prevented her from taking her

71

new musket to the ball, forgetting that she didn't yet know how to use it.

If he had heard her, Monsieur de Rouville did not let on. He did not raise his gun; instead, he in turn let out the night bird's sorrowful cry.

Two Indians loomed up before them. Her husband held her tightly by the arm. Was that to prevent her from crying out? He had nothing to fear. She wasn't the sort of girl to give in to hysteria. She was gathering all her strength and rage for one final combat.

Just then the clouds parted, and the moon cast its light on the scene, revealing the Indians' sharp features, the feathers in their hair and Monsieur de Rouville's calm face. He released his hold on her arm and raised his hand.

Speaking in a language she could not understand, the three men launched into a long conversation. Simon seemed to be giving instructions. He pointed towards the river, and the others responded by asking him questions. The discussion wore on, and Jeanne, drained of her energy by the sudden alarm and the day's emotions, was staggering with fatigue.

Without missing a syllable of his conversation, her all-seeing husband put a strong arm around her and held her against his hard body. She thought it was a gesture of tenderness and it moved her. But he gave her a little shake, as if he were bringing her back to her senses, then dropped her again. He didn't want to be dishonoured in front of his native friends by a weak woman. Jeanne stiffened. In the future she'd die rather than betray a single weakness.

After a final word, the Indians seemed to sink back into the night. She blinked her eyes and cocked her ears. She and her husband were alone again.

The iron fingers closed on her arm again and she was propelled forward in her lord's wake. A far cry from Lieutenant de Touron's respectful courtesy.

An instinct made Jeanne turn around. Once the danger was past, their two protectors had taken up their posts again. One was an Indian, the other walked with a limp. That was all she could determine.

A yellowish light in the window of the Bon-Secours School bore witness to Mademoiselle Crolo's zeal. The good lady sat by the hearth, saying her rosary, as she waited for her boarder. The new Madame de Rouville would sleep in the convent again that night.

Visibly preoccupied, Simon deigned to give her a brief explanation. "I have to finish my preparations. One of my men will come for you at dawn. Your trunk is down at the dock. Be ready. We'll be leaving very early."

"I'll be ready," she answered with dignity. A notion to rebel stirred under her calm appearance.

"Have you any more orders for me?" she asked impudently.

"Uh...no, madame," a surprised voice answered in the darkness.

"Then good night, husband. I'll see you tomorrow."

With dignity, the king's daughter closed the door in her hateful husband's face. For once she'd had the last word.

Jeanne curtsied to the sleepy nun. Then, without seeing one of its steps, she climbed the steep stairway. It was little more than a ladder leading to the attic of the stable they called a school—Sister Bourgeoys's pride and joy.

She held back her tears, firmly resolved not to let herself

be overcome by her emotions. Fortunately, Marie du Voyer, so sensitive and vulnerable, had been spared this ordeal. Jeanne Chatel was strong. Nothing would get her down. Stifling a sob, she pulled the blanket over her head and closed her eyes, determined to go to sleep. She would need all her energy to face the days ahead.

13

APPARENTLY the meaning of the word dawn varies from one continent to another. That was the conclusion Jeanne reached, snugly wrapped in her cape. It was pitch black. The now familiar whistle sounded under the window; she was ready. To be on the safe side, she had slept in her clothes. Her guide was a little grey-haired man whose toothless, wrinkled face was crowned by an enormous fur cap. His fringed shirt was black with the soot of countless campfires. He spoke little and had gathered all his courage to announce brusquely, "I am Mathurin the Limp. Monsieur de Rouville sent me to fetch you."

She blindly followed her limping guide. One of his ankles was twisted at an abnormal angle, which explained his nickname. Sometimes, when the path was rough, he used his long gun as a crutch, but his infirmity did not slow his pace. Jeanne puffed along behind him, thrown off balance by the heavy sack of medicines bumping against her side. Pierre Boucher had written in his book that "the Indian wife walked behind her man and carried the possessions." Jeanne was beginning to think this custom had spread to the whites, too. Fortunately she did not have much luggage.

The shawl, the white stockings, the shiny shoes and the

starched coif had disappeared into her huge pockets. Like a seasoned traveller, she had slipped on the thick woollen stockings, her old, indestructible shoes and covered her hair with a black scarf. In the shadowy light of the freezing dawn she felt pale and unattractive.

Fortunately, in the confusion surrounding the departure, her husband, gallant as usual, had no time to cast a look in her direction. However, he did not miss the opportunity to give out orders. He pointed to a large canoe already loaded with sacks and her trunk.

"Sit there on those blankets, madame, and don't move. We're crossing the river and any movement is dangerous."

I know that! Jeanne felt like shouting. Can you imagine, dear master, that I travelled by canoe for five days from Quebec to Ville-Marie without making it capsize?

Her revolt did not cross her lips. Coureurs de bois and Indians took their places in the eight canoes. She was the only woman, the only dead weight on the expedition, apart from the baggage that they nevertheless valued highly.

A tentative light rose in the east. The air was sharp and smelled of pine. Short, foam-crested waves stirred the river. Suddenly, an officer burst into sight on the road that led from the fort. He was running and waving his arms. It was Pierre de Touron coming to say goodbye, calling to them from afar.

Simon was sitting in the front of the canoe with Jeanne. He took the trouble to put on a friendly face, but he obviously couldn't resist a mocking joke.

"What heroism for a soldier of the king to rise so early in our honour!"

"I didn't do it for you," the officer assured him. He

turned to Jeanne. "I'm coming to present my good wishes to madame. You can get along very well without my blessing."

Suddenly growing serious, Monsieur de Rouville ordered him, "Tell de Preux that I...that we regret his absence at our wedding. As soon as he arrives, tell him I'll be waiting for him."

"I will," promised the lieutenant, who obviously was not insulted by Simon's commanding tone of voice. Why did Simon always have to address everyone as if they were his underlings, and why did no one—except for Jeanne—seem to take offense?

"We're heading out," announced the leader of the expedition, raising his paddle over his head.

Pierre bowed to the young woman. "Goodbye, madame. *Bon voyage* and *bon courage*."

"Thank you," Jeanne murmured, very moved.

She wanted to leap onto the dock, throw herself into the young soldier's arms and cry, "Keep me here with you. Don't let me go into the wilderness with all these silent men who don't even notice me!"

She tried to imagine the look on her lord and master's face if she were to make such a disastrous exhibit of herself. The thought made her lips curl into a spiteful expression. That was the image the admiring lieutenant was left with: a courageous woman going off to confront her destiny, a smile on her lips.

Without thinking, Jeanne waved farewell to him. Immediately from the front came a disapproving grumble.

"Don't move. I told you that before."

Jeanne looked at her husband's broad back blotting out the horizon and rebelliously stuck out her tongue at him, the noble Monsieur de Rouville.

14

NO one had bothered to inform Jeanne of the itinerary. Later she was to learn that this expedition the men were so eager to undertake was also a business trip, involving many detours and numerous stopovers.

Instead of heading towards Sorel and the mouth of the Iroquois River, the flotilla crossed the St. Lawrence at an angle and went down in the opposite direction. Jeanne stretched out and leaned comfortably against the bundles of furs and blankets. Her initial curiosity passed and she closed her eyes and fell asleep.

The burning midday sun awakened her. They were travelling along the deserted south shore of the river. She stretched as modestly as possible and turned to look back. The canoes were following as if they were being towed.

Mathurin gave her a wide toothless smile that made her laugh. At least he didn't ration his kindness.

In front of her, Simon was still paddling with the same regular motion, apparently tireless. She had the impression he could go on like that for days without feeling any fatigue. For a long time she examined what she could see of this stranger who was her husband. His well-muscled shoulders were held straight over narrow hips, and his long legs did not seem to suffer from their uncomfortable position.

He was sitting on the edge of his bench, with one knee on the floor of the canoe and the other bent in front of him, as if he were genuflecting. The musket he never parted with was lying beside his foot. Next to it was his wide leather belt with a dagger in its sheath, a well-sharpened hatchet and a curved horn containing his powder.

He was dressed in a soft leather suit, as he had been the day Jeanne arrived in Ville-Marie. His pants had long fringes along the sides of legs, and his shirt was decorated the same way, down the sleeves and on the sides. Later Jeanne would learn that these fringes were not simply for style. When it rained they allowed the water to drip more rapidly from the leather.

Simon wore his straight black hair too short for the fashion of the time. He probably doesn't know what a wig is, Jeanne thought. Despite the heat, he was wearing the inevitable long-haired fur cap that completed the uniform of every coureur de bois. On his feet were high moccasins that came up to his knees. The handle of a second knife was sticking out of the right shoe. You would have to wait a long time to catch that man without his weapons. He must be very familiar with danger.

Jeanne looked thoughtfully at the back of his shirt. The buckskin was still beige in colour. Was that because it was new, or simply cleaner than Mathurin's? Who had made that shirt and who had repaired the many tears in it?

A long cut with darkened edges zigzagged across her husband's right shoulder. Was that blood? The cut had been meticulously mended with thick black thread and small, even stitches. Discouraged, Jeanne once again realized she knew nothing about this stranger whose name she bore.

Just then, Simon, without throwing the canoe off balance, turned around in one lithe motion and looked her over. She was in for a shock. The eyes staring at her from that tanned face with its arrogant nose were green, a pale, limpid shade such as she had never seen before. Was it that contrast that gave his glance that icy, enigmatic appearance?

But his voice was cordial enough when he questioned, "You're not too tired, are you?"

Jeanne could not help laughing. "Tired? I'm the only one who isn't working."

Her logic caught him off guard. He said, "If you're hungry, open that sack on your right. You can drink the river water, but avoid sudden movements."

The noonday sun beat down on their heads. Jeanne carefully took off her cape and scarf and put her hand into the sack he had indicated. She took out a piece of bread and some venison that she devoured with gusto. Then she scooped up some water in the palm of her hand.

"Would you like anything?" she asked Mathurin. He shook his head and showed her something that looked like leather. He was chewing it, not at all handicapped by his lack of teeth.

"Pemmican," he explained, his mouth full. Jeanne recognized the food the Sulpicians had given to her on the way up from Quebec.

Simon put down his paddle and took off his fur cap. He pulled his shirt over his head and there he was, bare chested in front of his startled wife. Was this man completely uncivilized? Did he forget there was a lady present? Apparently so, since he plunged his paddle back into the water and broke into a stirring song in his strong voice.

À la claire fontaine
M'en allant promener,
J'ai trouvé eau si belle
Que je m'y suis baigné.

Mathurin picked up the tune in falsetto, and from the other canoes, the voyageurs joined in the choir. Jeanne had never heard anything as beautiful as this French song rhythmically sung by these rugged men as the canoes flew over the sparkling waters.

Timidly at first, then with greater assurance, she added her voice to the others. She sang well but too loudly, the nuns had always reminded her. Here the wind carried away her words. Absorbed by her pleasure, eyes lifted to the cloudless sky, she did not notice the questioning glance her husband shot in her direction.

Chante, rossignol, chante,
Toi qui as le coeur gai.
Lui y a longtemps que je t'aime,
Jamais je ne t'oublierai.

The sun struck the tanned back before her. The muscles rippled under his brown skin. On his right shoulder, a long scar traced the line of the tear in his shirt. Who had mended that tear? The same one who had sewn the clothing?

Cautiously, Jeanne bent down and picked up the leather jacket that had fallen at his feet. She examined the mending in the back and was not quite sure what to think. The seamstress had drawn the two sides of the tear together and sewn them with long, coarse black hair.

Lui y a longtemps que je t'aime,
Jamais je ne t'oublierai.

How far it was from the convent to Ville-Marie!

15

ON the first two evenings, the voyageurs put ashore near the charred ruins of small log forts. The canoes were beached and covers stretched over two of the canoes to make a shelter for Jeanne. Some of the men gathered wood and lit a fire. Others went off with their muskets and returned an hour later with game or a small deer.

It's hunting heaven, thought Jeanne. Grandfather should have built his paradise here.

Without a word, her husband disappeared with quick, silent steps, accompanied by a companion and one or two Indians. If he did not judge her worthy of his trust, she would certainly not bother him with any questions, Jeanne decided bitterly.

Fortunately, thanks to her usual warmth, she did not take long to overcome her travelling companions' shyness. They were paralyzed with respect for Monsieur de Rouville's wife. When they saw how lively, how curious she was about everything, ready to laugh at herself and others, these men of few words began to change. Campfire comradeship brought them together.

They answered her questions in great detail, interrupting each other, offering their knowledge of nature to this simple, natural young French woman.

A boy of her age, aptly named Carrot-Top, who came from Amiens, seemed to have devoted boundless admiration to Monsieur de Rouville. Jeanne learned some fascinating things from him.

"I came over on the same boat as the Builder. He was an officer and I was ship's boy."

"Who's the Builder?"

"Monsieur de Rouville—I mean your husband. He helped build nearly all the forts in the region. It's his specialty."

In strictest confidence, the boy added, "He was hoping to have this winter in peace at least. But Frontenac, the new governor, gave Cavalier de la Salle the job of building a fort on Lake Ontario for next summer. And as you might expect, de la Salle asked Monsieur de Rouville to get everything ready. The message arrived a week ago, and he was furious. He didn't cool down for two days. He was expecting you and that obviously wasn't what he had in mind. It's a bad set of circumstances."

"Couldn't he refuse?"

"Well, you see, madame, here in New France you don't refuse very much. Everybody has to do his share."

"And my husband's share is building forts?"

"That and chasing the Iroquois. They're scared to death of Ongue Hegahrahoiotie."

Intrigued, Jeanne tried to repeat the strange sounds.

"That means 'the man with the piercing eyes.' The Onondagas gave him that nickname."

For an instant Jeanne sympathized with the Iroquois.

"And you, Carrot-Top, what's your real name?"

He blushed and bent his fiery red head, digging his fingers into the pine needles. "Well, I don't really know. I'm a foundling, like they say. My father...I didn't have...at least, they don't know."

His voice broke during this incriminating admission. Now the pretty lady wouldn't look at him anymore, or she'd make fun of him like everybody else did, except for Monsieur de Rouville.

But Jeanne had inherited her grandfather's open mind. She repeated the same words her grandfather had used to silence his contemporaries' ill-natured remarks about illegitimacy: "Carrot-Top, the important thing is that you're here."

A confused expression spread over his freckled face. The boy's lips moved, repeating her words to himself. Then his face lit up, he raised his head and seemed to shrug a weight from his shoulders.

"That really is true. The important thing is that I'm here. That really is true."

Two minutes later, Mathurin, leaning against a tree trunk, ordered him, "Hey, Carrot-Top, go get another armful of wood."

"Go get it yourself, lazy bones," he answered, standing up to someone for the first time in his life.

His fists were clenched and his eyes were shining. Since he was strong and seemed determined, Mathurin gave up and went away with a shrug of his shoulders. Carrot-Top shot a triumphant glance at Jeanne; she was smiling. Never again would he be ashamed of his origins. No one would ever use that weapon to take advantage of him again.

In the evening, Jeanne would slip into her solitary shelter and roll herself up in her cape. She watched the dancing flames and listened to the whispering of the forest where her husband wandered as others would stroll in their garden. There he met friendly Indians, trappers and hunters, and set meetings with them for the spring.

The campers stood guard around her, sheltering her in the magic circle of their protection.

The voyageurs must have returned very late, because in spite of her vigilance, she never heard them arrive. At dawn, when she looked towards the glowing embers, she saw her husband and his companions stretched out on the ground. One day, perhaps, would the Builder take time to build his own home?

Finally the canoes turned around and went upriver. Still close-mouthed, Simon played the role of guide. With his powerful arm he pointed to a cluster of cabins on the shore and announced, "Longueuil!"

They stopped there for a night. Farther on was the domain of the Percee Islands that had been granted to Pierre Boucher, the author of Jeanne's bedside book. Unfortunately this busy man was away, and she did not have the pleasure of meeting him to congratulate him on his very interesting work. At noon, accompanied by a fine, stubborn drizzle, the canoes arrived at last at Fort Sorel, at the mouth of the Richelieu.

The night before, Carrot-Top had proudly explained to Jeanne, "It's one of the first forts the Builder and I constructed. That was in 1665. The old fort had been burned and Monsieur de Saurel asked your husband to help him. Monsieur de Rouville was still young, but he was already a commander. All the men obeyed him. He was a captain in the militia back then."

"But you must have been a child!"

Carrot-Top was very proud of himself. "I was already twelve years old. I'd been following Monsieur everywhere for two years. He took me off a boat where they were mistreating me. I was strong already and I could do my share. So when he said to me, 'Come on, Carrot-Top, we're going to build a fort for Monsieur de Saurel,' I went. I'd follow him to the ends of the earth and so would everybody who knows him."

Not so fast, Jeanne thought, though she kept it to herself. There's someone here who'd be a little more reluctant. Yet she had to admit bitterly to herself, What do you think you're doing right now, poor little fool, if you're not following that man to the ends of the earth?

The garrison at Fort Sorel gave Monsieur de Rouville and his companions a joyous welcome.

Standing beside her husband, Jeanne watched him searching for something while he answered the local dignitaries' questions.

He finally managed to get away and whisked her off to a little log house nestled against the wall. He walked quickly, and once again Jeanne had to trot along behind him. He stopped at the threshold and rapped sharply on the door. His frown and his black look did not augur well for those who were slow to answer.

The door opened timidly. Then a fat woman wrapped in a dirty apron appeared, blocking the doorway.

"Where are they?" Simon asked roughly.

"I wasn't expecting you so soon," mumbled the matron.

"So I see. Where are they?"

Reluctantly, the woman stepped aside and pointed to the

dirty interior of her miserable cabin.

"Go in. They're there. I took good care of them as you..."

Without bothering to listen to the rest, Simon bent his head and stepped through the low doorway. Jeanne hesitated, then followed him. Two frightened children were waiting, standing by the window. The boy put a protective arm around the little girl. They were dirty, thin and dressed in rags.

Without a word, Simon knelt down and examined them. With his finger, he stroked the little girl's chin and the boy's tousled hair.

From the door, an overly sweet voice ordered, "Children, bow to your father."

They bowed obediently, without changing their expression. Jeanne, who had lived among orphans, felt her heart fill with pain to see the fear and passivity written on their unhappy faces.

Simon, still kneeling, turned his anguished face towards her. She read so much distress in his pale eyes that, for the first time, she felt compassion for that proud, hard man.

In a low voice, he tried to explain, "You see why...you understand why I had to..."

What she saw and understood was the need to find a new wife for Monsieur de Rouville. A devoted person, anyone at all, to get the children out of that situation as quickly as possible.

Simon stood up and said suddenly, "Nicolas, Isabelle, this is your new mother."

"Hello, ma'am," murmured the boy. His distrustful green eyes looked up at Jeanne from under a fringe of black hair. He was five years old, but he seemed much younger.

Isabelle, two years his junior, held out a timid hand to Jeanne. In an unsteady voice, she murmured, "Mama?" as if she were learning a forgotten word all over again.

Unable to speak, Jeanne dropped to her knees and opened her arms. Compassion melted her reserve, as it had in the past with Sister Berthelet. The children snuggled against her and spontaneously, Jeanne pressed the thin little bodies to her breast. Though they could not have said why, they knew they would never be alone again.

Simon contemplated the scene a moment and his eyes filled with tears. Then his anger took the upper hand. Enraged, he turned on the terrified shrew.

"I'm taking them away. Pack their things!"

"I didn't have enough food, sir...I had to—"

"You sold everything? But I paid you more than enough. Never mind. Come, madame. Follow me, Nicolas and Isabelle. We're leaving."

Two little hands held on tightly to the king's daughter's fingers. She went out, head high, the two children right on her heels. Monsieur de Rouville brought up the rear, musket in hand. In his eyes all the problems had been solved. He had reunited his family and life was returning to normal.

His responsibilities as the Builder took over immediately. He was very much in demand. Almost embarrassed, he handed Jeanne a few silver coins.

"Perhaps you can find them some clothing with this. I have to leave you for the day...I'll come back at nightfall."

Faced with this typically masculine attitude, the young wife shrugged her shoulders. Obviously she would do what was necessary, but a father got off easily.

All afternoon, she made use of her reserves of energy and

her storehouse of persuasion to wash the children, comb their tangled hair and get warm, clean clothes for them. In a country where everything had to be hand-sewn, and where nothing was thrown out that might be saved and made into something else, buying anything new was out of the question. A pair of pants here, a shirt there, stockings somewhere else—little by little she gathered together outfits that were comfortable, even if they did not fit very well.

The children, dazzled by their new elegance, hardly dared to stir. Isabelle's blonde curls peeked out from under a pretty blue bonnet, and Nicolas's straight black hair disappeared under a magnificent fur cap similar to his father's. In the course of her comings and goings, Jeanne did not neglect to consult the fort's official "healer." She was a fine old woman, only too happy to entrust Jeanne with her secrets and give her curative herbs that would add to the medicines provided by Sister Bourgeoys. This slip of a woman could do a world of good with her beautiful smile and her remedies.

When evening came, Simon found all three of them sitting around a campfire, devouring the rabbits, killed and prepared by the Limp, as if they had been starving to death. The old trapper had known the children since they were in the cradle, and he was touched to see them again. "It was a shame to watch them wasting away with that witch," he said to Jeanne. "But she was the only woman who would agree to look after them. People here have enough to do with their own brood. Monsieur was worried to death, and he was looking forward to your coming."

Unwittingly rubbing salt on the wound, Mathurin added, "It won't be long before they accept you as their mother. You look enough like her to be her sister. Fate has her ways sometimes, doesn't she? The very night you arrived, Simon said to me, 'Limp, it's as if Aimée came back.' He's mighty lucky to have found two like that in one lifetime. Mighty lucky."

Monsieur de Rouville took one look at his transformed children and exclaimed, "I hardly recognize them. Madame, you have worked a miracle."

Jeanne smiled modestly, holding back all the acid remarks on the tip of her tongue.

Simon stayed just long enough to get his family settled for the night in the attic of the blacksmith's house. Then he was off again, leaving Jeanne to sleep with, literally, an armful of children.

16

IF this young, inexperienced mother had feared for her children on the canoe trip, her fears were quickly dispelled. Nicolas and Isabelle were true settlers who knew that staying perfectly still was the rule when on the water.

The little girl stretched out at Jeanne's feet. For hours she watched the sky without moving, and the rest of the time she slept.

In a different canoe, Nicolas was also quiet and calm. They were so good they worried Jeanne; at that age she would not have had the same capacity to remain quiet.

An Indian woman with a pack on her back was standing motionless at the intersection of a little river. At a signal from Simon, Carrot-Top paddled the canoe to the shore, and the woman got in without word. Nicolas gave a shout and raised himself onto his elbows.

"Gansagonas!"

"Quiet," his father immediately ordered. Passively, the child lay down again and fell silent.

"Who is she?" whispered Jeanne, too intrigued to wait any longer.

Without turning around, Simon hastily answered under his breath, "The Huron woman who brought them up. They haven't seen her for a year."

The cruelty of this separation and her husband's callousness made Jeanne indignant. After all, he was depriving the children of the joy of a reunion. Again she had to remind herself that this cruel and threatening world spared only those who respected the laws of silence and prudence. The sooner the children learned these harsh lessons, the greater would be their chances of survival.

The sun had disappeared behind the tops of the pines when someone called to the voyageurs from the shore.

"Hey, Rouville! Welcome! We've been waiting for you."

A new log wall held court in the midst of a clearing: Fort Chambly, erected in 1665 by the same crew that had built the one in Sorel. The Builder, known everywhere, awaited at every stopover, was welcomed with open arms. This time, his good friend Captain Hubert de Bretonville was the official host.

Simon jumped onto the crude dock and shook the captain's hand. Then he turned and helped Jeanne, who was always stiff by the end of the day.

With a proprietary air, Monsieur de Rouville introduced her: "This is my wife, Jeanne. Captain de Bretonville was in the same regiment with me in Europe."

"My very best to you, madame. I'll be pleased to tell you anything you'd like to know about your husband's wild youth."

The captain burst out laughing at the sight of Simon's sombre face. "Look at him seething, madame. I've got him at my mercy and I'm going to take advantage of that to extract all kinds of favours from him. The first one is to have the honour of your presence in my house."

"But the children, monsieur," Jeanne objected, quite at sea.

"Of course, the children. Believe me, it's high time they had a home again. My wife is waiting for all of you at our house."

De Bretonville took Jeanne familiarly by the arm and led her through the humble cabins of Chambly. Nicolas and Isabelle ran alongside and clung firmly to her skirt. They had found security, and they weren't about to let it escape. Though they had kissed Gansagonas, the Huron woman who was following right behind them, even she didn't make them forget their new mother.

A few ladies were enjoying the cool of the evening on the steps in front of their open doorways. "Oh, what beautiful children!" exclaimed one of them, full of friendly curiosity. "Are they yours?"

"Yes, they're mine," answered Jeanne instinctively.

She turned to look at Simon; he had a contented smile on his face.

Poor Aimée, thought the king's daughter. How quickly she has been forgotten and replaced. Jeanne held the children's hands tightly; full of remorse, she felt as if she were robbing a dead woman.

The arrival at the captain's house was straight out of Homer. Tiny, plump Thérèse de Bretonville twirled around in a flood of welcoming words. She disposed of everyone in short order.

"Simon, dear, go into the living room with Hubert. Smoke your awful pipes and have a drink together. You can relive your mad youth. Madame, I'm keeping you here with me. It's been too long since I've talked to a real French woman. This is my sister, Nicole. She'll look after the children. Come, my darlings, Nicole will give you some dinner and show you our little puppies. They're adorable, really adorable."

Her head spinning, Jeanne didn't quite know if it was puppies or children under discussion. She was afraid of disappointing this charming lady who obviously thought Madame de Rouville was a woman of the world, full of the latest gossip.

Thérèse flung one last order over her shoulder to make sure she hadn't forgotten anyone.

"Your people can eat and sleep in our common room and Gansagonas will find her compatriots in the kitchen. Come, my dear. I'm going to show you my castle."

Jeanne had nothing to worry about. Even if she had known all the scandals of the court, her hostess babbled on so much that she would not have been able to tell about a single one. The house was modest, though larger and more comfortable than any Jeanne had seen since she arrived.

"My father is very rich," Thérèse confided, with no pretense of humility. "He spoils me."

"You have beautiful furniture," her visitor was able to get in admiringly.

"Yes, it's true. It took us four years to have everything brought over from France. No doubt they'll feed the next fire the Iroquois set. In the meantime I like to see them here."

This fatalistic reminder of the constant danger hanging over the isolated forts did not seem to depress the irrepressible Thérèse.

She led her guest into a large, well-lit room dominated by a huge bed. Thanks to her hostess's organizational talent, the king's daughter's trunk had already been taken there.

Jeanne gratefully accepted the offer of a hot bath.

Two Indian women brought the water from the kitchen.

An hour later she came downstairs, her hair still damp, curling around her tanned face. A white collar and leather shoes supplemented her outfit.

The meal was sumptuous and gay, more abundant than any she had ever experienced before. The silver plates and crystal glasses made her forget the wilderness outside. The impeccable service provided by the Huron women added an incongruous note to the feast.

Jeanne sat opposite her husband, carefully noting which utensils he used, and picking up the same one in return. Simon, very much at ease, had obviously lived in such luxury before. The conversation revealed new aspects of the Builder's character.

When he realized Jeanne knew nothing about her husband, Hubert decided to enlighten her, despite Simon's meaningful glances.

Simon de Rouville was the eldest son of a rich and important family. Like many adolescents his age, he had joined King Louis XIV's army when he was very young. The impetuous young man had provoked a duel with a relative of the king; unfortunately, he was adroit enough to wound him.

"Immediately afterwards, the young charmer who had caused all the drama showed a deplorable lack of logic and married a third person. Your husband was left brokenhearted, disinherited and exiled. France's loss was the colony's gain."

When the meal was over, Thérèse took Jeanne to kiss Isabelle and Nicolas goodnight. Glowing with happiness, the children insisted on taking the puppies to bed with them.

Thérèse left the men to enjoy their brandy, and she went to sit at the foot of her guest's bed. It was the time for advice and confidences.

"I would gladly have looked after the children, but I was in France the year of the tragedy. When I returned I was very sick, even if I don't look it now. Since then I've been travelling a great deal with Hubert."

Obviously quite pleased with the situation, the chatterbox added, "My husband takes me everywhere with him. Of course he's no backwoodsman like Simon..."

"I hope you'll have better luck keeping your husband at home than that poor Aimée did. If he stopped travelling about the country so much, he could be prosperous. You know, you remind me a lot of Aimée."

Without noticing the pained expression that came over Jeanne's face whenever that hated comparison was made, the thoughtless woman rattled on, "Yes, there really is something of Aimée about you. But you're more alive."

I should hope so, Jeanne thought, amused in spite of herself at Thérèse's involuntary macabre joke. Her sense of humour made her appreciate all the subtlety of Thérèse's slip of the tongue, but at the same time she was inwardly revolted by it.

Must she always be the pale reflection of another women? Would anyone ever recognize eager, spirited Jeanne behind Aimée's borrowed face?

Finally Thérèse noticed Jeanne stifling a yawn, and left her for the night.

Jeanne was happy to find herself in civilization again.

She put on her vast nightdress and, delighted, slipped between the cool sheets. Never before had she slept on a feather mattress. She got up again, climbed onto the foot of her bed and, arms spread, she let herself fall. It was like sinking into a cloud. The candle on the night table cast dancing shadows on the walls.

Forgetting her age and the dignity of her position, like a school girl on vacation, she repeated her little trick. All alone, laughing, drunk with freedom, she got up and let herself sink down. Never again could anyone tell her to be reasonable.

A slight noise made her turn around. Leaning against the closed door, Simon was contemplating her with a surprised look. Jeanne pulled herself up, her cheeks on fire. This big devil of a man had walked in as noiselessly as an Indian and caught her right in the middle of acting childish.

Furious, Jeanne tried to regain a semblance of dignity. "What are you doing here, monsieur?" she asked haughtily.

Simon gave a quiet laugh. "It seems I have come to watch Madame de Rouville frolicking about."

"Monsieur, I am afraid you may be disappointed with the wife the king sent you."

With one eyebrow raised sarcastically, he retorted, "I didn't expect anything good from the king. I must say I misjudged him."

Simon went to the mirror and took off his shirt, the famous leather shirt mended with one long black hair. Again she thought of the French beauty who had been the cause of a duel, his pretty cousin Marie du Voyer whom she'd replaced, and Aimée whose place she was taking. Bitterness filled her.

Why love life so much, why long for love so much, when you're living out someone else's life? She blew out the candle, buried her face in the pillow and burst into tears.

When she sensed Simon's silent presence by the bed, Jeanne burst out between two sobs, "Go away. I hate you. I'm not Aimée and I never will be!"

A few seconds later she heard the door close quietly. Then her tears flowed harder still.

17

THE stopover in Fort Chambly lasted three days. The first morning Simon appeared before his wife, holding their two muskets.

"Come," he commanded. "You must learn how to use this weapon."

He took her behind the fortifications, placed some apples on stakes for targets and began the lesson. As her husband's strong arms held her to direct her fire, Jeanne thought, How he must wish I was Aimée.

She made rapid progress, which seemed to surprise her teacher a great deal. He wasn't expecting very much, she said to herself spitefully.

As they were returning to the fort, Jeanne leading the way, they met the same inquisitive woman who had asked whom the children belonged to that first evening. Deciding, no doubt, that she was entitled to one question a day, she stopped in front of Jeanne.

"Tell me, my dear, what is your name?"

"I am Jeanne Chatel, madame."

"Jeanne de Rouville," corrected a mocking voice behind her. She quickly turned around and met her husband's cold eyes.

Very spritely, her words heavy with hidden meaning, she

replied, "You're right. I am Jeanne de Rouville. Sometimes I forget."

The gossip hadn't dared hope for so much. To her great joy, Simon turned on his heels and walked away, whistling to himself.

Sarcasm, thought Jeanne. Two can play that game. It seemed to her that many of their conversations ended with one of them stalking off.

At Jeanne's request, Thérèse introduced her to old Hippolyte, who was known throughout the region for his healing talents. The white-bearded old man reminded Jeanne very much of her extraordinary grandfather—the same inquisitive mind, the same realistic philosophy. There was an immediate understanding between these two very different people. For hours, Jeanne added to her brand-new knowledge of medicine, scribbling precious notes in Sister Bourgeoys's little book.

The healer examined the contents of her sack. He added numerous other plants and roots, and advised her how to find and use them.

"Spruce gum is the best antiseptic and should be gathered during the full moon. Gall from a male bear cures bronchitis in women; only gall from the female can cure men."

Jeanne was taking the mission entrusted her by Marguerite Bourgeoys very seriously.

That same evening, the last one of their "vacation" in Fort Chambly, the hosts gave a dinner in honour of the newlyweds. If anyone noticed a coldness in their marital relations, they didn't let on.

Thérèse came and knocked on her guest's door.

"Jeanne, you seem to have only dour, dark-coloured dresses. Let me give you one of my sister Nicole's outfits; she's the same size as you. It's time your husband discovered the pretty woman under that nun's frock."

Blushing but grateful, Jeanne accepted the kind offer. Madame de Bretonville was excited about her own idea and proceeded with the transformation.

Jeanne wondered what role she would play this time as she went down the stairs to greet the guests. Her hair was styled in the latest fashion—at least it had been the fashion two years before in France—very prettily swept up on her head. The blue silk dress, lighter than any material the orphan had ever seen, emphasized her generous bosom and her fine waist. The gold medal gleamed from among the soft folds of a chiffon scarf. She took a step forward, tottering a little on the high heels Thérèse had insisted she wear with the dress. Very proud of her work, Madame de Bretonville followed her guest.

Simon was waiting at the foot of the stairs. He had put on his wedding suit, which lent him a civilized air, despite his dark complexion and overly short hair.

He was talking to Hubert and two officers in uniform when he absent-mindedly looked up. There was the new Jeanne descending the stairs.

Monsieur de Rouville stopped in the middle of a sentence; his mouth fell open. Very pleased with her entrance, Jeanne raised her chin and tried on a coquettish smile for the first time in her life.

I'm one of the ladies of Versailles, she thought, very satisfied with herself. All I need now is to provoke a duel between my impetuous husband and an officer and I'll have my patent letter of nobility. What would my father, the king, have to say about that?

Alas! even coquettes have to watch where they put their elegant little high heels. With a loud scream, Jeanne toppled forward in a spectacular tumble. Her last hour had come. She closed her eyes and thrust her hands out.

Simon leapt forward with unbelievable speed, as swift as a beast of the forest, pushing aside Hubert and his guests. He caught his wife in his outstretched arms, though she was tumbling head first, and managed to break her fall. With trills of sympathy, the startled ladies surrounded the victim, thinking she had fainted.

Pressed against her husband's chest by imprisoning arms, her head buried in his sturdy shoulder, Jeanne trembled uncontrollably. Simon bent over her, concern written on his face. Torn between worry and relief, and impatient, too, at these feminine indispositions, he gave her a little shake.

"Come now, madame, you've been saved. There's no need to panic."

Unable to speak, Jeanne threw back her head and clung to his wedding suit. Abashed, Simon discovered his wife wasn't crying. Far from it. She was laughing so hard she could scarcely catch her breath.

"My father...the king...my father...the king," she finally hiccupped.

"She has lost her reason," the ladies concluded.

Jeanne shook her head, still laughing. Her entrance into high society had been a great success. She met Simon's puzzled green eyes and burst out laughing once more.

Seeing that, her lord and master set her on her feet none too gently, but kept his arm around her waist just for caution's sake. The proud Builder didn't like to be ridiculed, and his sombre expression made that very clear.

Thérèse, the perfect hostess, appeared with a glass of Spanish wine.

"Drink this, Jeanne. There's nothing like it for restoring the equilibrium."

Madame de Bretonville definitely had the knack of making puns in spite of herself. Whipping the whole agitated group into shape, as was her wont, she went on, "Come, ladies, follow me. Hubert, it's time to go to table. Simon and Jeanne will join us. Drink up, Jeanne, drink up."

Urged on by this barrage of instructions, the group broke up, leaving the king's daughter and her husband alone. He was still holding her close and, doing as she had been told, Jeanne swallowed the soothing wine in one gulp.

She did not dare raise her eyes to the man who was waiting stiffly at her side. What must Monsieur de Rouville think of that ridiculous scene? If only she had had the presence of mind to feign a swoon. A defenseless woman is forgiven everything.

Simon shook her again, none too gently. She had given him a fright and he held that against her.

He whispered angrily, "You silly fool. Don't you even know how to walk down a flight of stairs?"

"I'm not a lady," Jeanne protested, lowering her head.

An authoritative hand lifted her chin and domineering lips claimed her mouth. True to form, Simon kissed as impetuously as he mounted an offensive.

Without giving her time to collect herself, he turned her around, took her by the arm and propelled her towards the dining room. There the guests greeted them with the jokes that suited the occasion.

Intoxicated by the wine—and perhaps by the kiss—Jeanne enjoyed herself. Her joyful laughter rewarded those fellow diners who paid her clever compliments.

Questioned about her journey across the Atlantic, the storyteller from the orphanage came back into her own. She amused everyone with her picturesque descriptions and anecdotes. Forgetting the discretion, reserve and self-effacement preached by the nuns, the old Jeanne Chatel reappeared, exuberant and full of fun.

Her liveliness fell on fertile ground. Here was a gathering of optimistic people who faced death and lived intensely. They had no time for affectation; her freshness cheered them up. The conversations were animated, the atmosphere relaxed.

Thérèse, very proud of her protégée's success, smiled maternally. Hubert stole a glance at Simon. Perhaps this time his friend had finally found a suitable wife. But he didn't seem too convinced of it yet.

Monsieur de Rouville was sitting at the other end of the table, thoughtfully observing the surprising wife the king had sent him. And several times Jeanne felt his green eyes upon her.

Unfortunately, everything comes to an end. The guests left, and Hubert went out on the doorstep to see them off. Thérèse disappeared for a final inspection of the kitchens.

Simon was in the hallway, bending over a table topped by a decorated mirror, checking a long list he had taken from his pocket. He seemed preoccupied. There were so many essential things he had to think about before he disappeared into the depths of the countryside for the long winter.

Jeanne, still excited by this unforgettable evening, carefully picked up her skirts to climb the stairs. Her lord's commanding voice stopped her on the second step. Without turning around, he issued his orders.

"Madame, we're leaving at dawn. Don't forget. Make all your preparations and be ready."

Already he was buried in his papers again.

Jeanne made a mocking pretense at a curtsey and murmured, "Very well, my lord." Then, like an incorrigible child, she stuck out her tongue at the broad back before her.

Suddenly she froze. Above her husband's shoulder, she met a pale, icy stare in the mirror. He had seen her.

He set his papers on the table, turned around and in two steps he was beside her. She waited, holding her breath.

"Madame, you are an impudent girl."

He picked her up in his arms as if she were Isabelle, bounded up the stairs and, with his shoulder, pushed open the door of the room with the big feather bed. He closed it behind him with his foot. His eyes were shining like emeralds in his tanned face.

Carried away in a whirlwind, Jeanne thought that nothing and no one could resist him. Simon set her down on her feet by the bed—gently this time. He held her curly head firmly in his two big hands. Never would she have believed those pale eyes could express so much tenderness and gentleness. Once again she trembled under his unending kiss.

18

THE canoe glided through the autumnal forest. New France was putting on its most beautiful finery. A radiant sun lit up the trees, whose magnificent colours enchanted the king's daughter. This was the season the settlers had baptized "Indian summer."

Silent, as were all men of the woods, Monsieur de Rouville enjoyed Jeanne's enthusiasm. He was proud of his adopted country's beauty and possessive of every tree, every changing aspect of the river they were ascending. At times Jeanne felt he had invented the entire landscape just to present to her as an offering.

They travelled in short stages, interrupted in the evening by the forays Simon and his men made into the forest. Now, however, Simon would return sooner and slip quietly into the shelter the Limp faithfully constructed for Jeanne. She slept in her husband's powerful arms or stretched out beside his slender, muscled body, as safe as in her garret in Troyes.

The muskets were always within reach and the knife was stuck into the ground near their bed of branches. But it wasn't the weapons that reassured Jeanne. In her husband she felt a strength and a will that left no place for fear. Now she understood Carrot-Top's declaration: "I'd follow him to the ends of the earth and so would everyone who knows him."

The children slept with Gansagonas, who cared for them with silent devotion. The young dog that the Bretonvilles had given Nicolas complicated things in camp.

When the little boy had appeared on the dock, rubbing his sleepy eyes and dragging a puppy as wide as it was long on a leash, Jeanne saw Simon's face grow hard. She guessed a refusal was about to follow, if only as a matter of prudence. With a courage that was new to her—for she had grown up in submission—she stood up to authority. She borrowed Thérèse de Bretonville's favourite tactic and let fly with a barrage of orders in all directions.

"Nicolas, did you thank the captain for his gift? Keep the dog next to you. Gansagonas, show him how to keep the animal quiet if he has to. Come sit beside me, Isabelle. You'll see the dog tonight. Mathurin, is my medicine bag in the canoe? Good, then we can leave. Goodbye, Captain."

She slipped into her place in the canoe and waited to see what would happen. Simon turned around and stared at her, open-mouthed. The expression on his face was one of profound amazement.

Then he shrugged his shoulders, raised his paddle and all the canoes glided over the water. Hubert, thinking it was too good to be true, waved to them from the shore.

Jeanne was in the midst of savouring her triumph when her husband turned around again.

"God preserve me," he grumbled under his breath. "I've married a shrew."

"And I a despot," the rebel retorted sharply.

Simon took up the task of paddling again, and a few

minutes later, Jeanne noticed his shoulders were shaking convulsively. His head thrown back, Monsieur de Rouville was laughing as if he didn't have a care in the world. She was carried along by his infectious gaiety, and both of them shared the joke for a long time, united by a new friendship.

At the rear of the canoe, Limp, his toothless mouth opened in a wide smile, turned to his right.

Carrot-Top's canoe was gliding parallel to him, a few feet away. The two coureurs de bois exchanged a meaningful glance. It had been a long time since they had heard monsieur laugh. It would be a good winter.

19

ONE morning, after days of travelling and numerous detours, the little boats approached the shore near a small clearing. Simon jumped into water up to his knees, and in one movement he pulled the canoe onto a sandy beach. He lifted up Isabelle at arm's length and set her on the bank. Then he picked up Jeanne in the same fashion and whirled her around.

She'd never seen her husband so exuberant.

"Here it is. This is my estate," he announced.

Where? What estate? Jeanne wondered, but she was tactful enough not to show her disappointment. Some estate indeed!

Simon took her by the hand and proudly showed her every inch of it. There was a field as big as the deck of a ship, the blackened ruins of a house and, beside it, a ten-foot-long dwelling made of round logs and lit by a doorway with an animal skin for a door.

"Before, it was just forest," he said proudly, pointing to the clearing.

But it's still forest, Jeanne thought, her heart softening. And far from fearing that hostile presence that encircled them, she loved it. Among those reassuring trees she was rediscovering all the joys of her youth.

Simon led her to the burned-out house. "You won't be afraid to live near these ruins, will you? It's temporary, you understand."

"But I spent my entire childhood in ruins like these," she exclaimed with a laugh.

Seeing her husband's perplexed expression, she added smartly, "I'll explain that to you later."

They still knew nothing about each other, but they had a whole life time to remedy that ignorance.

The sight of his burned house must have brought back painful memories to the lord. His mouth took on a bitter curve and his eyes misted over with sadness.

The Builder's friends had helped him construct a comfortable home in the middle of the forest for a spoiled girl who would accept nothing less. Simon rolled a piece of charred wood with the toe of his moccasin.

Jeanne felt pity for him, but at the same time a voice inside her cried out, You can see perfectly well that he hasn't forgotten a thing. He still misses her and he's searching for her everywhere, even in you.

It is difficult to believe in happiness when you have been deprived of it for so long. Simon and Jeanne often fell back into the insecurity of their past lives.

But they were both people of action. Jeanne turned towards the log cabin. "Is this where we'll live?"

Simon was a little embarrassed. He thought of Aimée's whims again.

"Yes. I was hoping to have time to build another house before you arrived, but I wasn't able to."

"In New France you don't refuse very much. Everybody has to do his share," Carrot-Top had said. And apparently her husband's share was to build for others.

"Now it's too late for this winter. We'll have to live here," continued Simon. "Do you think you can?"

With an effort he added, "If you prefer, I can have you taken back to Chambly with the children, or even to Ville-Marie. Before now I never realized how crude this shelter was. I'd built it for myself after...when..."

For the first time, Jeanne witnessed her husband at a loss for words. He was nervous, and he studied her anxiously. Surprised, she realized he seemed to be waiting for an outburst, a wave of protestations. Perhaps Aimée had conditioned him to recriminations and tearful scenes.

Faced with the prospect of a winter in that primitive structure, Jeanne couldn't blame the poor woman, especially if she had been accustomed to an easy, ordered existence. But judging by the size of the ruins and the remains of the chimneys at each end of the blackened rectangle, the house where Rouville had brought his first wife had been quite large and comfortable.

Once again, the king's daughter was thankful that fate had sent her here, and not the fearful Marie. This country was definitely no place for a lady. However, for an orphan girl brought up by a poacher, it represented an exciting challenge. Monsieur de Rouville would see that his wife's rustic character had some redeeming factors.

Jeanne turned to the man anxiously watching her and declared, "You'll be surprised to learn that I haven't always lived in luxury either. If we must spend the winter here, then it's high time we start preparing for it."

With a determined wave of her hand, she brushed aside the fur pelt blocking the doorway. Her firm voice showed she was taking the situation in hand.

"To begin with, we'll need a suitable door, with a solid beam to barricade it."

She continued her inspection in the dim light while Simon, leaning against the doorway, watched her with fascinated eyes.

"We'll need a table here near the hearth and two benches. Shelves here, and there and there. And in this corner"—she kicked at a pile of branches and old pelts—"in this corner, a good solid bed. Later you can give me a feather mattress," she added without blushing.

Simon slipped behind her, laughing, and put his arms around her waist. His nose against her neck, he murmured, "There's no doubt about it, I married a shrew. An adorable shrew."

"Windows. I'd like windows. I need light."

Her husband looked gloomy. "In New France, windows are hard to come by. I could make an opening, but it would have to be boarded up as soon as it gets cold."

"I'll think of something," promised Jeanne, the incurable optimist. "Can you make a platform at this end with a ladder where the children can sleep, like at the blacksmith's house at Chambly?"

The young woman went about the cabin, organizing, making plans. She asked, "Where will Gansagonas live?"

"She'll prefer a shelter next to the house. The Hurons hate living in our houses. And Limp, too, for that matter. He'll build himself a cabin near the river."

"And Carrot-Top and the others?"

"They'll be off in the forest hunting and trapping all winter. That's the season when the pelts are at their best.

112

They have contracts with the traders in Ville-Marie who finance their expeditions and supply them with ammunition, provisions and blankets. In exchange, the trappers bring their furs to their warehouses."

Suddenly Jeanne had an intuition. "And someone has financed you for the winter, Simon?"

Embarrassed, he looked down at his hands, then raised his head and returned her gaze with his pale eyes. Nothing and no one intimidated Rouville for very long.

"Well, yes! I have trading contracts to respect, too, before I leave on an expedition to Lake Ontario."

"Then you're going to have to be away and leave us alone, the children and me? Why didn't you tell me?"

All of a sudden Jeanne felt betrayed, caught in a trap among the threatening trees of the encroaching forest.

"But I thought you knew. You saw the preparations I made. Everybody here knows I'm a trapper, not a farmer."

Everybody but his wife, who is far too trusting, Jeanne thought bitterly.

Then she raised her chin with a determined air. "I'll find a way to manage by myself."

"You won't be alone. Limp and Gansagonas's brother Anonkade will stay with you. They'll hunt and cut wood and in case of attack..."

He did not finish his sentence. As she had told Marie in her letter, Monsieur de Rouville had no intention of losing another wife at the hands of the Iroquois.

"If you must leave us so soon," said Jeanne, just a trifle sharply, "all the more reason to begin making the repairs to the house as quickly as possible."

Monsieur de Rouville didn't have to be told twice. After

all, the scene he had feared had gone very well. He would be spared the crying and tears that used to accompany each one of his departures. One day, as his friends had advised him, he, too, would spend months improving his property. Meanwhile, the forest awaited him, mysterious and dangerous. He still did not know how to resist its call.

20

SIMON wasn't called the Builder for nothing. With his axe he expertly fashioned the door, shelves and furniture Jeanne had demanded.

Limp was a big help, despite his infirmity. They both hunted and smoked meat for the winter. With the aid of Jeanne and Gansagonas, they harvested the enormous pumpkins growing in the small field between the stalks of Indian corn. At the end of the summer, Limp came to gather the ears of corn for Simon and stored them in the "cellar" behind the cabin.

This cellar, a small eight-foot square underground room dug directly into the earth, was reinforced with tree trunks and lined with fir branches. It was used as a pantry and a cache for fur pelts. Sealed by a trap door and hidden under a square of turf, it was absolutely invisible to anyone who did not know of its existence. It was an undertaking of which Simon was very proud.

The two men stored supplies of dried corn, smoked eel and pumpkin in a chest. Set near the hearth, it would serve as a pantry and would contain the family's staple food during the winter. The fruits of the hunt completed this frugal diet that was shared by all the settlers in the colony at that time. Molasses and raisins brought by boat from the West

Indies were the only sweets that broke the dullness of these monotonous meals.

From morning till evening the king's daughter, sleeves rolled up on her strong arms, washed, scrubbed and brought order to the dark cabin.

One way or another she got everyone settled. She put a mattress filled with leaves and moss on the rope bed. The patchwork bolster given to her as a wedding present by Madame de Bretonville livened up the "bedroom" corner with its bright colours.

On the rough table she placed the blue-flowered sugar bowl that Thérèse, seeing her admiration for it, had generously given to Isabelle.

In the corner near the hearth, the wooden trunk Louis XIV had given his "daughter" did double duty as a storage space and a seat.

The iron pot, essential for any cook, hung on the chimney hook that Simon had been farsighted enough to bring along in his baggage.

On the wall near the door, wooden racks awaited the muskets that the settlers hung up as they came in, above the powder horns and sacks of lead shot.

Branches of autumn leaves, changed every day, were hung above the table, adding an artistic touch.

A broom made of twigs attached to a handle vigorously swept the dust from the beaten earth floor.

Next year, Jeanne planned, without a doubt to trouble her, I'll ask for a wooden floor. No, why not a whole new house?

Meanwhile, in her energetic grasp, the log cabin became a warm and hospitable home.

When the principal furnishings were finished, Jeanne attacked the next problem. The children were so out of the habit of laughing and so uprooted that they sat in a corner for hours without moving. The harpy who had looked after them had terrorized them. Their big serious eyes followed the young woman's every movement; the puppy was the only one who seemed to be enjoying his childhood.

Perplexed, the inexperienced mother studied the problem. Suddenly she had an inspiration.

In a spirited voice she announced, "Now, the most important thing is to make a doll for Isabelle and a ball for Nicolas. Come and help me, children."

From the king's daughter's trunk, Jeanne produced two pairs of white stockings that were part of her trousseau. Sitting on a log in front of the doorstep, she opened the sewing kit Mother de Chablais had given her before she left.

With a malicious smile the good nun had said, "I know that using a needle and thread is not your favourite activity, my daughter, but the day will come when this kit will make you a perfect housewife."

The Mother Superior disguised her nagging doubts with a commendable optimism.

Little by little a doll took shape, thanks more to the seamstress's ingenuity than her deftness with a needle. The excited children gathered dead leaves to stuff it. Growing lively for the first time since Jeanne had known them, they gave her advice in their serious voices. Jeanne, as much an instinctive psychologist as Sister Berthelet, led the children to take part in the operation.

"We need some hair. What will we use for hair?"

"What about mine?" Isabelle suggested timidly.

Nicolas solemnly cut off one of his sister's blonde curls, and the doll got its head of hair. A fringe borrowed from the Spanish shawl became a smiling mouth. For the eyes, Jeanne sacrificed—with no regrets—two of the blue buttons from the silk dress Thérèse had forced her to take along in her trunk. They dressed the doll in a flowered handkerchief, a present from Mademoiselle Crolo upon Jeanne's departure from the Bon-Secours School.

Wild with delight, Isabelle pressed the shapeless doll to her heart.

"What will you call her?" asked Jeanne, threading her needle. "A name is very important for a girl."

"Her name should be Aimée," Nicolas decided, making Jeanne's heart seize with pain.

"No," decreed Isabelle, contradicting her brother for the first time. "She's mine and her name is Zeanne."

Tears in her eyes, Jeanne kissed the little girl's blonde head.

"And what about me?" cried Nicolas without ill will. "What about my ball?"

They set to work again. Once more, a stocking and some leaves made their contribution. Artistically decorated with carbon, saffron and a few drops of blood—for the unskilled seamstress pricked herself often—the ball was thrown and caught with cries of joy. Unfortunately, its career was almost cut short; the dog got hold of it and ran off with this toy that had fallen from the sky into his clutches. An epic pursuit, punctuated by cries and laughter, ended in the capture of the ball.

"Bad dog," scolded Nicolas. "He doesn't come when I call him."

"That's because you haven't found a name for him," explained Jeanne. Out of breath, she let herself drop onto her log.

"Call him Zeanne," suggested Isabelle, who had a one-track mind.

"Silly. That's no name for a dog. Mama, what's a good name for a dog?"

"I once knew a boy whose name was François. He had a dog called Miraud," said Jeanne dreamily.

"Then my dog's name is Miraud. Come, Miraud. Here, Miraud."

For safety's sake, Jeanne tied a long string to the ball and fastened it to a branch. She was quickly discovering parental tricks for avoiding difficulties.

Happy with her success, she watched the children playing. A new idea came to her suddenly. Too long absent and awkward with the children, Simon was a stranger to Nicolas and Isabelle. She had to remedy that. Immediately she began a clever campaign to bring them together.

"Children, when your papa comes home, you must show him your new toys. Papas are very interested in their children's games. He'll be very pleased."

She watched for Simon and ran to meet him when she saw him coming out of the forest, gun in hand, a haunch of venison over his shoulder. Surprised and touched by this welcome, he gave one of his rare smiles, revealing his sparkling teeth that had the power to make Jeanne's heart melt. She trotted along by his side, very lively, absorbed by her own plot.

"Simon, you'll have to be very interested in what the children are going to show you. It's very important to them."

"I'm afraid I'm not a good father."

"But you can learn to be. You see, I wasn't a lady either but I learned."

That flash of wit made the hunter burst out laughing. Still holding his musket, he wrapped his arm roughly around her.

"Indeed. To look at you with your cap all askew, your sleeves rolled up and your nose all dirty, it's plain to see you're the mistress of a lord who wears a wig."

Jeanne's innocent ruse bore fruit. As Simon sat on the log carefully cleaning his gun, Isabelle timidly came near, holding her doll.

"Her name is Zeanne and she's beautiful."

"Look, sir," cried Nicolas, punching the ball with his fist.

The young father put down his weapon and sat the little girl on his knee. He examined the doll seriously and had her tell him the long story of its manufacture. Little by little, Nicolas, more daring, came closer.

"My dog's name is Miraud," he said. Then the child mustered his courage and mumbled, "May I look at your gun, sir?"

Busying herself over her pot, Jeanne followed the events, a smile on her lips.

When Simon came in to eat an hour later, he lifted Nicolas up in his arms. The little boy, proud as punch, hung the musket on the rack near the door all by himself. As soon as his father set him on the ground, he ran over to Jeanne.

"Mama, Papa is going to take me into the forest tomorrow. And later Miraud is going to be a hunting dog. Isn't that what you said, Papa?"

"An excellent hunting dog, no doubt about it. Probably the best in Canada and maybe in all of New France."

Laboriously, Isabelle explained, "Sir Papa, he's going to make a cradle for Zeanne with boards, and it'll rock and Zeanne will go to sleep and..."

Over the children's heads, Simon and Jeanne exchanged the amused glance of indulgent parents.

The young woman rejoiced. Her cabin in the woods had become a happy home, the home of Jeanne de Rouville, king's daughter and mistress of the manor.

21

DURING a family stroll in the surrounding forest, Miraud flushed out a partridge.

Nicolas, a lively child, ran ahead of them, exclaiming, "Look, the bird is hurt. Its wing is dragging and it's walking all crooked."

Simon was a hunter who appreciated the value of any game he saw, and he had already shouldered his gun.

Jeanne gently turned the muzzle of the gun aside. "Don't shoot, Simon. It's a poor mother protecting her little ones by pretending she's hurt. She deserves to have her life spared. She's a heroine."

"How do you know that?" asked Simon, who persisted in thinking his young wife was a townswoman.

"When I was young I learned that from my grandfather who was a poa...I mean a hunter like you. Look, children, the little partridges are hidden here. Let's leave them in peace."

A conscientious teacher, she explained the mother partridge's clever trick to the fascinated children. She walked down the path, holding Nicolas and Isabelle by the hand, and captivated them with her well-told story. Simon followed her, shaking his head. His second wife never ceased to amaze him.

Walking along a barely visible path, they stopped near an enormous tree that towered over all the others. To have room to grow, it was not adverse to choking or crowding out its neighbours.

Simon pointed it out. "That's the old giant, the biggest oak in the forest."

Adjusting his musket on his shoulder, the hunter stretched out his arms, made a leap and caught hold of a branch. Pulling himself up agilely, he hoisted himself into the tree. They watched his leather-clad figure disappear higher and higher between the bare branches.

Craning her neck, Jeanne asked, "Why are you climbing? Is that your chateau?"

Childhood souvenirs crowded her memory. Perhaps even serious adults needed a land of dreams.

The lord's distant voice reached them. "It's an excellent observation post. From the top I can see both sides of the river."

He came down rapidly, with sure movements, bombarding them with broken twigs.

Like an expert, the young wife observed his manoeuvres. Nose in the air she said admiringly, "You climb well for your age."

Simon stopped short and contemplated her there at his feet. "What do you take me for, your father?" he protested.

Candidly, Jeanne let herself be carried away once again by her indiscreet tongue. "Not all forty-year-old men can climb so fast," she stated with conviction.

"Forty years old?"

As if in shock, Simon let himself slide down, straddling a branch. Incredulous, he repeated, "Forty years old? Where did you hear that I'm forty years old?"

Jeanne regretted her remark. Too late, she realized she must have wounded him. And she'd even sworn to herself never to refer to their age difference.

Leaning over her, Rouville repeated, "Who told you that?"

"Carrot-Top did. He didn't say that exactly, but he told me you were building forts in 1665 and that you were a captain. Hubert de Bretonville is a captain and he's more than forty. So...I thought..."

Embarrassed, she stammered and fell silent.

Like a cat, Simon jumped down beside her. He looked at her, head bent, fists on his hips.

"Madame made clever calculations. Madame drew conclusions. You silly little thing. I was a captain in the Canadian militia, not in the army. And in New France we're not very old when responsibilities are thrust on us. I'm old, that's true, older than you. I'm thirty-two years old, not forty."

With great dignity he turned and strode away, pursued by Jeanne and the children. From time to time they heard him mutter, "Forty years old. An old husband. Imagine that!"

For the hundredth but not the last time in her life, Jeanne resolved to hold her tongue and turn it around a good number of times in her mouth before speaking.

Just the same, she was happy to have made a mistake in her calculations. Simon was much younger than she had thought. That meant they would be together longer. She would have to tell him that, whisper it in his ear that evening. That would console him.

Her peace of mind restored, careless Jeanne recovered her good mood and whistled like a bird.

Simon, still surly, turned around brusquely. A lady whistling?

"Where did you learn to do that?"

"To imitate birds? My grandfather showed me. I have all sorts of hidden talents."

He was beginning to suspect as much. That's exactly what was worrying Monsieur de Rouville. For the past few weeks, his life had been more full of the unexpected than on an expedition to Huronia.

22

ON a dull day at the beginning of November, a canoe passed on the river, and its passengers hailed Simon, who was cutting wood in front of the house. Picking up the rifle next to him, he went down to the river bank and chatted with the voyageurs for a long time. All the news of the area, transformed, exaggerated or embellished, was exchanged and commented on. Then the canoe moved on, and Rouville came running back to the house.

In spite of the cold, the door was wide open to let in the pale autumn sun. Singing, Jeanne was making the dust fly with an aggressive broom.

"What is all this housewifely fury?" exclaimed her husband, always surprised by the energy his wife expended in everything she did.

"This floor is impossible to keep clean. I'd like a wood floor."

"You won't have it this year, but you might find something you like at the Quatre-Ruisseaux fair."

He had the satisfied look of someone with a surprise up his sleeve. His curious wife jumped at the bait.

"What are you talking about? Don't be so mysterious."

"Come on, we're going shopping."

"Simon, you're dreaming. What do you mean?"

"Every year, before they leave for the winter hunt, the settlers, trappers and Indians get together where the four streams meet. For a few days, a great exchange of goods is made. Everyone brings a few things he doesn't need anymore."

"What is surplus for some brings happiness for others," Jeanne concluded.

"Exactly. Dress warmly and put the things you want to get rid of in a bag. I'll tell Limp about it and I'll join you at the canoe."

As excited as a small-town woman who has been promised a day in the Paris boutiques, Jeanne turned circles searching for unneeded possessions in her humble abode.

She finally chose the last pair of white stockings, and after much hesitation, she threw in the blue silk dress. It was already wrinkled and too beautiful for life in the forest. After all, I can bring it back if I don't find anything I like, she reasoned, justifying herself.

Simon made her sit in the bottom of the canoe and covered her with a bearskin.

"When will you teach me to paddle?" she protested. "I feel like a useless burden."

"This isn't the time to risk being capsized, not in this icy water. In the spring I'll show you how."

He still considers me a precious doll, Jeanne lamented.

Despite her efforts, the shadow of Aimée, ineffective and timorous, was hanging over their heads. Simon, the strong and competent protector, still nurtured a false, chivalrous idea of women's helplessness in the wilderness. To keep from disappointing him, Jeanne had not yet dared to enlighten him.

For the young woman who had lived in solitude for weeks, the scene at the Quatre-Ruisseaux fair presented an extraordinary spectacle. About fifty trappers, settlers and Indians had placed the oddest assortment of objects on the ground, and they were doing their utmost with word and deed to attract the attention of potential customers. Except for Jeanne and a few Indians, there were no women. The strangest thing was that, instead of the cacophony that should have accompanied these exchanges, scarcely a murmur of conversation was heard. The Indians and coureurs de bois did not quickly break their customary silence.

"Tonight," Simon predicted, "when the whiskey is passed around, it will be a different story. But we'll be gone by then. Do you see anything you like?"

"Not so fast. I want to look everywhere."

Eyes shining, like a child in a candy store, Jeanne ran from one spot to the next. Her indulgent husband let her go and went to chat with some old fellow adventurers.

Two hours later, he looked around for his wife and found her. She was radiant. She showed him the fruit of her transactions lying at her feet: a cast-iron frying pan with a long handle and, miracle of miracles, a round-topped door whose upper part framed an unbroken glass pane. The two objects must have changed hands many times.

"That's my window, Simon. I have a window!"

Simon turned to a coureur de bois behind him. "You see, Charron? What woman wants, woman gets. Are you happy? Nothing else you need?"

"I have nothing more to trade."

"Then let's go."

All of a sudden Simon looked concerned and cast a questioning glance around.

"What's the matter, Simon? Are you worried?"

"It's nothing. I thought I saw some fellows I had some misunderstandings with."

Charron, who was listening to them, leaning on his musket, cut in with a short laugh.

"Misunderstandings. He calls them misunderstandings. Damned Rouville!"

Turning to Jeanne, the man spat on the ground and proceeded to tell some secrets. "Rouville caught those bandits selling fire water to the Indians. He nearly killed one, beat up the other and made them lose their fur trading permit. You don't call that a misunderstanding. Damned Rouville! He'll never change. Always be a fighter."

"I'll see you at Katarakoui, Charron," Simon interrupted with a frown.

He wasn't at all anxious for his wife to learn of the ups and downs of his stormy career. Picking up the glass door and adjusting his rifle, he turned on his heels with dignity.

Jeanne, clutching her heavy frying pan, had to run to keep up with him, as usual.

"What's this Katara something or other?" she asked.

"Katarakoui," Simon flung over his shoulder. "It's the name of a river we're going to explore with Cavalier de la Salle, on Lake Ontario."

"Not so fast, Simon. Wait for me. I don't have long legs like yours."

They were going down the slope that led to the canoe. Suddenly, without a sound, a man appeared on the path. He had an axe in his hand and was brandishing it threateningly.

"Goddamned Rouville!" he shouted, blocking the way. "I've been waiting for this moment for a long time."

Sure of himself, the man was already savouring his revenge. He hadn't counted on his adversary's reflexes. With lightning speed, Simon let the precious door slide to his feet, grabbed his musket by the barrel and in the same lithe movement, turned it around, hitting his aggressor right in the jaw as he was preparing to lower the murderous axe.

Just then, a big blond-bearded fellow appeared on the path, bent double, his hand clutching his knife as if it were an extension of his arm. He didn't look as though he would make the same mistake as his accomplice.

Simon's hand slid towards his moccasin, and when he straightened up he was holding his knife like a man who knew how to make use of it.

It all happened so quickly that Jeanne was left standing stock-still in surprise. She heard footsteps behind her. Someone jostled her and a third man, also armed with an axe, ran past. Leaping like a wildcat, he jumped on Rouville's back and wrapped his legs around his waist. Savagely, he grabbed hold of Simon's hair and pulled his head back, exposing his defenseless throat to the blond giant's weapon.

In a gasping voice Simon ordered, "Jeanne, run to the fort. Quickly."

He bent forward, trying in vain to dislodge the man straddling him.

Galvanized into action by her husband's order, Jeanne awoke from her lethargy. An unspeakable fury seized her at the sight of those murderers threatening her happiness, ganging up to attack Simon.

Brandishing the heavy frying pan over his head, she measured the distance and brought the utensil down with all her might on the head of the man holding the axe. He slid to the ground, limp as a rag.

Rouville didn't lose any time trying to find out how he was released. A fierce and seasoned fighter, he leaped head first onto the surprised bearded man. The two of them rolled on the ground and fought in a silence more threatening than any scream.

Of equal strength, each in turn took the upper hand. Strong wrists stopped the knife thrusts, and in the tangle of arms and legs, Jeanne could not tell who was her husband and who was the enemy.

But she was far from being a passive spectator. The dangerous pan raised in her hand, she moved around the combatants, waiting for her chance to intervene. A gasp for breath, a grunt of effort, a muffled curse were all that broke the silence.

Suddenly, with a prodigious arching of his back, the bearded man took the upper hand. He raised his knife. At the last minute, Simon intercepted the threatening wrist and stayed it.

Jeanne seized her opportunity and lowered the avenging pan a second time.

Alas! At that very instant Simon made a desperate recovery and dominated his adversary. The pan struck his dark head with a dull thud. Like a sledge hammer, Monsieur de Rouville collapsed on top of his enemy. The latter jerked, cried out and moved no more.

At the sight of those two motionless men, Jeanne's fury evaporated. She dropped her all-too-efficient club and fell to her knees by her husband. Grabbing him by the shoulders and pulling back with all her might, she managed to roll his large inert body onto its back. Simon's eyes were closed. Blood was running from the corner of his mouth.

"I've killed him," Jeanne murmured despairingly. She shot a quick glance at the bearded man. He was staring up at the sky, his own knife buried in his chest.

Trembling, Jeanne pressed her ear to her husband's leather shirt. All she heard was the wild beating of her own heart.

A shadow blotted out the sun; she looked up. Instinctively her hand closed over the familiar handle of the frying pan. No one would touch her husband's body as long as she was alive.

The rough voice of Charron the trapper remarked, "A fine slaughter. With Rouville it's never anything else. Is he dead?"

"I think so," Jeanne murmured in a broken voice.

"He's often looked dead but it's never happened yet," he commented philosophically.

He put his ear to his comrade's chest, raised his head, spit to one side and assured her, "No deader than I am. Is he hurt? A knife in the back, by any chance?"

She hardly dared admit it. "No. A frying pan. I hit him on the head by mistake."

Charron broke up laughing. He said, "Rouville has a hard head. It would take more than the bottom of a pot to finish him off."

Picking up the weapon responsible for the crime, he weighed it in his hand and disappeared into the trees. Two minutes later he returned, carrying the pan full of water. He emptied it onto the injured man's face. Simon groaned and opened glazed eyes.

"Simon!" cried Jeanne. Now that the danger was past, she burst into tears.

Charron rummaged unceremoniously through the dead man's pockets, mumbling, "He always had some on him, the dirty bastard."

He produced a bottle of brandy and roughly lifted Simon's head. Simon let out a groan and grimaced. Without pausing to sympathize, the trapper poured a good ration down his throat.

Rouville coughed, spat, choked and found himself sitting up, gasping for breath. He grabbed hold of the bottle with a firm hand and took a long drink, his head thrown back. He seemed to have forgotten his wife was there, still sitting on her heels behind him. When his eyes fell on the corpse beside him, a string of abuse issued from his lips.

Charron gave what he thought was an unobtrusive jerk of his chin in Jeanne's direction. Surprised, then embarrassed, Simon stared at her. Had she understood his colourful language? Apparently so, since a mocking glint lit her tearful grey eyes.

Intrigued, Simon touched his skull and considered his bloody hand.

"Were they everywhere? Was there a fourth one?"

Jeanne blushed while the trapper choked with laughter. He pointed to the frying pan and explained, "You have a wife who knows how to handle a pot. If I were you I wouldn't contradict her too often."

Jeanne became suddenly busy, wrapping her handkerchief around her victim's head. Charron examined the other assailants and came back to them.

"I'd get going before these bastards come to. There might be other...misunderstandings. Come on, I'll give you a bit of an escort. Pick up your things."

"My window!" Jeanne cried, bounding over to the door. It was intact. With great care she picked it up and held it in front of her leaving her husband to get up as best he could by holding onto a tree.

Charron retrieved the musket and slung it over his shoulder next to his own. Then, still laughing, he put the frying pan into Simon's shaky hand.

"Carry this, Rouville. If anyone attacks you, you can defend yourself."

And that's how Jeanne found her glazed window and Monsieur de Rouville, the dreaded Ongue Hegahrahoiotie of the Iroquois, returned home lying in the bottom of his canoe, clutching his head in both hands and fortifying himself from time to time with a mouthful of medicinal brandy.

Meanwhile, Charron, in fine humour, taught the pretty Madame de Rouville how to paddle a canoe. He predicted a brilliant future for her on the rivers of Canada.

23

FAITHFUL to his promise, Simon took his son on a short excursion to hunt for small game. The child, armed with a wooden rifle skilfully carved by Mathurin, went off proudly, an empty sack over his shoulder. With his fur cap and fringed leather suit Gansagonas had made him, he was a miniature replica of his father.

At the end of the day, the hunters returned, triumphant. Simon walked along in long, easy strides, forcing Nicolas, exhausted and burdened by the big sack overflowing with hares and partridges, to run along at his heels. Too tired to eat, the child, still proud as punch, fell asleep with his nose in his plate. His father laid him on the straw bed in the loft and covered him carefully with the bearskin blanket.

"You're asking too much from him," Jeanne took him to task. She was beginning to think her projects for bringing father and son together had their less desirable side.

"Set your mind at ease, Mother Hen, I'm not the brute you think I am. I carried both the hunter and the game most of the way back. But that, obviously, was to be kept secret. When we reached the old oak we both assumed our roles again. He'll be good in the woods," Simon concluded, pleasantly surprised at his discovery.

"Who could he have gotten that from?" Jeanne retorted

teasingly, an innocent look on her face.

The next day Simon and Anonkade, the Huron, left, this time to bag a moose. Monsieur de Rouville wanted to smoke a lot of meat for the winter. The expedition was to last two days or more, depending on the luck of the hunt.

Abandoned and disconsolate, Nicolas watched them go. His little form, topped by the enormous fur cap, looked ridiculously like a large mushroom. Jeanne's heart softened. Miraud sat whimpering next to his young master; he seemed as disappointed as Nicolas that he could not follow the hunters. Gansagonas had been gone since dawn gathering certain dried herbs and roots found only at that time of the year. Jeanne was planning to get an explanation of their properties during the winter, when the intimacy of the warm house would melt the Huron woman's reserve and overcome her exasperating silence. Limp was away; he'd gone with Carrot-Top, who had come to borrow him for a few days.

Jeanne was making corn cakes with her usual vigour. Every bit as busy, Isabelle put her doll to bed in the cradle Simon had built her. Zeanne, warmly covered with a rabbit skin Gansagonas had tanned, was listening patiently to the endless stories her young mother told her.

At noon a delicious smell of warm cakes filled the cabin. Jeanne opened the door and called Nicolas, who was a great trencherman. Mealtime always tore him away from his fascinating games.

This time the child did not appear when she called. Even the shrill whistle that usually made Miraud come flying home produced no result.

Worried, Jeanne circled the house, musket in hand.

With a sinking heart, she went to the river bank. The canoe was there, but not Nicolas. Even if the little boy had hidden out of spite because he had not been invited to go hunting, his still undisciplined dog would have answered Jeanne's whistle, since she always had delicious surprises in store for him.

In real anguish she dressed Isabelle, put on her grey cape and, with the loaded gun over her shoulder, started along the path, calling and stopping frequently to listen. Soon she had to carry her tired daughter in her arms. With this burden, Jeanne visited all the familiar places where Nicolas might have taken refuge.

At the foot of the big oak, full of hope, Jeanne lay Isabelle in her cape; the little girl had fallen asleep. Remembering the escapades of her youth, she decided to climb once again. Perhaps Nicolas had a ship or a chateau up there, despite his young age. She did not see how he could have reached the first fork. It was even out of her reach, but you could expect anything from ingenious Simon's son.

And from his wife, too. Jeanne had soon leaned a big dead branch against the trunk. With all the agility of a ten-year-old girl, the poacher's granddaughter confidently climbed the tree. A familiar longing filled her and made her forget for a moment why she was climbing. From the top she saw the brilliant ribbon of the river winding in the distance, curving in front of the Rouville property. She had to face the facts: Nicolas could not be in the oak tree.

Disappointed, Jeanne resumed her search. Twice she returned to the cabin in hopes of finding the repentant runaway there. Around five o'clock she met Gansagonas coming home through the woods, loaded down like a mule.

The Huron woman met the news of Nicolas's disappearance without batting an eyelash. She set her burden down, bent over the path, inspected the underbrush and announced haltingly, "No tracks. Dead leaves hide. Evening come. We go home."

She took Isabelle firmly from Jeanne's arms. The little girl had been crying softly for hours, aware of her adoptive mother's nervousness.

But Jeanne, exhausted, could not persuade herself to abandon Nicolas. She pictured his frail little form, his pale eyes so like Simon's. A fine rain began to fall, and the thought of the child alone in the terrifying forest filled her with horror.

She left Gansagonas and Isabelle in the cabin, slipped a few cakes and a piece of cold meat into her pocket and went out into the twilight. A sudden inspiration made her climb the old oak once more. Clinging firmly to the highest branch, she took a shot into the air. She reloaded it as quickly as she could in her unstable position and fired two more shots. She hoped from that height the echo would not be muffled by the trees and would carry her call for help to the hunters.

Before climbing down again she nibbled on a cake, pulling up her hood for shelter from the persistent rain. Where could a little boy hide, disappointed at being left behind? Trying to remember her own childhood, Jeanne thought long and hard.

Suddenly she remembered the very deep ravine they had walked along one day with Simon. Pointing out the depths of the abyss one hundred feet below, he had said,

"Sometimes in the winter, moose and deer fall into this hole and sink into the soft snow. You find their skeletons in the spring."

Could it be that Nicolas, who never missed a thing, had decided to go all by himself to look for a moose of his own? Jeanne picked her skirts up and ran through the trees, hurrying before the darkness fell completely. Confident that she would be able to get her bearings in the woods—as she had done so many times at her grandfather's side—the imprudent girl didn't think of her own safety or the hazards in the Canadian forest, much more dangerous than the overgrown estate in Troyes.

Carried along by her zeal, she nearly fell head first into the very ravine she was looking for.

Her musket caught on a branch and stopped her, one foot dangling in space. Far below, she heard the stones she had dislodged falling down the slope.

She leaned over the abyss and called again, "Nicolas, Nicolas!"

Her clear voice echoed and re-echoed in the night, tipping off the Indians—if there were any—that a foolhardy white woman was near.

Now Jeanne gave the low whistle that always brought Miraud running. From the distance muffled barking reached her ears, barely perceptible. Straining her senses, she repeated her call and heard the same response. Miraud was somewhere below at the bottom of the ravine, and Nicolas, too, most likely. Perhaps the little boy was unconscious or injured, or even dead. Shuddering, Jeanne pictured—as if it were there before her—the little lifeless body, shattered on the rocks.

Her eyes had grown accustomed to the darkness, and now she made out the bushes and rocks strewn here and there on the steep incline. She would have to take this hazardous path. What about the musket? Burden herself or abandon it? The danger below was not the type you confront with a weapon. Agility counted now.

She hung the gun on a branch and pushed back her cape, heavy with rain. Then she turned around, got down on all fours and slid backward down the slope that grew steeper and steeper. The wet branches slipped through her grasping fingers, and stones rolled from under her rough shoes and cascaded beneath her skinned knees. Often she slid flat on her stomach, desperately trying to break her fall. It seemed to her this descent into the underworld lasted for hours.

Her hands bloodied, face scratched, hair standing straight up, she found herself on her knees at the bottom of the ravine. Her ears were filled with the sobs of her own laborious breathing. Painfully rising to her feet, she whistled again, softly.

The stifled response came to her from so close by that she jumped in terror. In the blackness she heard Miraud's tail thumping and the dog's desperate efforts to reach her. The string with which Nicolas held him in the woods to keep him from chasing rabbits must have been caught somewhere.

Guided by the sound, she went forward, hands stretched out before her, dragging her feet on the ground. She stumbled on rocks, stepped over fallen tree trunks and caused a small nocturnal animal, just as surprised as she was, to scurry away noisily. Miraud whimpered constantly, directing

140

her blind search.

Finally she reached him near an enormous dead tree. As she had suspected, the string was wrapped around a branch. His warm tongue licked her face and hands as, on all fours, she groped around the dog, calling softly, "Nicolas. Where are you, Nicolas? Don't be afraid, it's Mama. Nicolas, answer me."

"Mama," murmured a small trembling voice.

Jeanne cried out joyfully and wrapped her arms around the frail little form lying between two rocks.

"You're hurting me," he groaned tearfully. "Mama. I don't want to go hunting anymore. Take me home."

By a stroke of luck, the moon came out just then, casting a vague light on the bottom of the abyss. Even the moon's rays were filtered down there. Making her hands as light as possible, she examined the child from head to toe. He was soaking wet, feverish and, judging from his moans and the angle of his wrist, he had a broken arm. Jeanne knew very well that moving him before daylight was out of the question. With determination, she got busy preparing for their vigil.

Once more she put to use one of the six large handkerchiefs from her trousseau. Louis XIV would be delighted to know how useful his gifts were, she thought, as she made a splint with straight branches and the square piece of cotton. She tore off a corner of her skirt and wiped the child's burning face as he clung to her. She pushed aside the branches of a dead tree near where Nicolas had rolled, and she discovered a relatively dry spot under this makeshift shelter. She set the injured boy inside in her cape; now she was thankful for its cumbersome size.

Imitating Gansagonas, she folded a leaf and patiently held out her hand in the increasing rain. She collected a few drops of water to quench the child's thirst. They shared the remaining corn cake and the cold meat; Miraud had his share, too.

Then Jeanne called the dog, who came to press his body against them. All three huddled together in the king's daughter's cape, almost frozen to death, waiting for daybreak. At times Nicolas was delirious; at others he trembled with fear. In a low voice Jeanne told him all the amusing stories in her repertory. Soon the child's curly head fell heavily onto his mother's enveloping arm. Jeanne counted the hours, listened to the rustling of the shadows and, in spite of her worries and discomfort, rediscovered the serenity of a night in the forest she had loved so much.

She forgot her resolve to stand fiercely on guard. She, too, fell asleep, exhausted.

This was the touching scene Simon discovered in the morning: his wife and son, dirty and covered in blood, asleep in each other's arms. Miraud, the only one in good shape, did not budge. He seemed to know it was his job to keep them warm.

Alerted by the distant gunshots, the hunters had scoured the woods all night. Daylight enabled them to make out tracks, and the musket hanging on a branch led the rescuers to the bottom of the ravine.

Anonkade climbed up with Nicolas strapped on his back. Simon pushed and pulled Jeanne to scale the steep cliff; her agility surprised him. In broad daylight, overcome by vertigo, she was thankful the darkness had hidden the dangers of the descent the night before. Her husband insisted on carrying her in his arms all the way to the cabin. And even if she was fully capable of making the trip on foot, Jeanne let herself relax against his strong chest, listening to his wildly beating heart. For the first time in her life, she said to herself that there must be some advantages to being weak and defenseless. Since that was how Simon persisted in thinking of her, she would play the role successfully—more or less.

Impassive, Gansagonas greeted them in front of the door.

"She was very worried," Simon assured his skeptical wife. Could he read the Indian's innermost thoughts?

Jeanne dipped into her big bag of medicines and prepared a sleeping draught for Nicolas. Helped by Simon—who was pale under his tan—she reset Nicolas's wrist and fashioned a splint with some small boards that looked almost as professional as the ones Sister Bourgeoys made.

Assured of his family's fate, and seeing Limp return from his excursion, Monsieur de Rouville went off again. With the Huron on his heels, he went to get the meat from the moose they had killed the previous day.

24

FOR two days Simon, Mathurin and the two Hurons had been smoking meat in a cabin prepared for this job behind the house. All four were bustling about, and they turned down Jeanne's help.

Isabelle was sleeping and Nicolas, still feverish, was lying on the big bed with Miraud. It was one of those surprise days the autumn sometimes has in store for Canadians, when a summery sun sends out its warming rays.

At loose ends, since she didn't dare make any noise in the house, Jeanne went to sit by the water. The calm river reflected the bare trees. Only a few obstinate leaves brightened up the dark wall of pines.

The canoe was lying upside down on the shore. Brimming over with energy, Jeanne decided to put trapper Charron's paddling lessons discreetly into practice. No sooner thought than done.

The bark canoe was easy to turn over and push into the water. Following the advice she had been given, Jeanne took off her shoes. She left behind her cape that was too warm but, as Simon always did, she laid the inevitable musket at her feet in the bottom of the canoe.

A dexterous young woman, she remembered the instructions she had received and the easy movements Simon made as she watched him during their travels. Soon the canoe was moving forward, turning and going backwards, passively obeying the slightest dip of the paddle. It was really very simple; she didn't see why Simon had made such an effort to keep her from learning. She moved out towards the middle of the river. If her husband could see her now, he would leave behind his ridiculous prejudices. She steered the canoe towards the shore and looked up. Simon was just coming around the corner of the house, his axe over his shoulder.

Jeanne raised a triumphant hand to wave to him. With no further warning, the canoe, once so passive, tipped over, sending its passenger into the icy water.

Her air cut off, she kicked her feet to resurface. Since she was eight, she had been swimming in the big pond in the Troyes forest. Contrary to what people thought in those days, her grandfather considered swimming an essential and healthy exercise. It is an art you do not soon forget.

The canoe was floating, half submerged, a little farther on. Something hard brushed Jeanne's leg on its way to the bottom.

My musket! thought Jeanne, horror-struck.

That very precious weapon was irreplaceable. Gathering her courage and her breath, she dove after the gun. Fortunately, her already numb fingers closed over the barrel on her first attempt. Relieved, she came up and decided to swim to the canoe and push it to shore, not far away. She would get off with a cold and a scolding from her angry husband.

Just then she spotted him running down the slope, throwing aside his axe, musket and fur cap. He flew to her rescue, not realizing she was in no danger and could rescue herself very well.

As he ran, he shouted his encouragement, and his booming voice reached her ears.

"Wait for me, Aimée. I'm coming!"

Jeanne felt all her strength leave her. Gently she slipped under the icy water, pulled down by the weight of the gun she refused to drop. Her long, untied hair floated out behind her, and before her open eyes, the water grew darker and darker. She wanted to die. She was already dead. The man she loved preferred a memory to her.

An iron hand grabbed her arm, pulled her out of the water and held on to her securely. Unable to resist, the musket between her hands, Jeanne let herself be pulled to shore. Simon roughly turned her over onto her stomach and administered two resounding slaps on the back, making her cough up water.

He was so worried about her he had not even noticed his unfortunate mistake. He picked her up in his arms and ran towards the house, calling loudly for Gansagonas.

Still not responding, Jeanne let herself go, wondering if that was what death was like. Her sinking heart pained her, and her constricted throat let not a word escape. Her heavy limbs hung limp like those of Isabelle's doll.

Helped by Gansagonas, to whom he gave brief orders in her own language, Simon undressed Jeanne and wrapped her in the quilt.

Galvanized into action by Simon's instructions that were spiced with oaths, Mathurin lit a gigantic fire in the fireplace. Simon set his inert wife in front of the flames and covered her with all the furs in the house. Usually so dexterous, he upset the pot of warm water and alcohol he was heating. He forced the liquid between her blue lips. Soaked to the skin, he forgot that he, too, was shivering with cold.

He bustled about, vigorously rubbing her frozen hands and feet.

He muttered between his teeth, "Silly little fool. You gave me a terrible fright. And you didn't even let go of that damned gun that was dragging you down. Jeanne, don't ever do that again."

He called her "Jeanne" now, absolutely unaware of the cry that had escaped his lips in a moment of stress.

Close by her, Jeanne heard frightened little Isabelle crying and Nicolas asking in a choked voice, "She's not dead, too, is she?"

Moved by the children's despair, she turned her head with great effort.

"Don't cry, my darlings. I'm fine now."

At least those two needed her, even if she was just a borrowed mother for them.

For Simon, she was and would remain the copy of the wife he had lost. Aimée had lent her her face, her children, her house, but even in death she jealously held on to her husband's heart.

Tears ran slowly down Jeanne's pale cheeks. Kneeling beside her, Simon cradled her in his too strong arms and whispered tender words in her ear. Weary, she turned her head away and refused to listen to those words of love meant for someone else. With the same sensation she had felt when the icy water drew her towards the refuge of forgetfulness a short while before, she fell into a dreamless sleep.

25

ON the first day of December, four large canoes halted in front of Monsieur de Rouville's domain. Carrot-Top, some Hurons and trappers were coming to get their hunting companion for the winter expedition.

The Richelieu's swift current made the river navigable, but very soon ice would set in for many months. Then the voyageurs would abandon their canoes for snowshoes. After the spring breakup they would take to their small boats again. The rivers were still the best routes for the rapid transport of furs to the warehouses of Ville-Marie and Quebec.

Recent treaties with the Iroquois raised hopes for a time of peace. The coureurs de bois were less fearful of disappearing into the forest and leaving their families for several months.

With shouts and laughter, the men cheered Simon and greeted their old friend, Limp. Since his accident, he had had to give up going with them.

Simon, the fate of his wife and son assured, waited on the river bank, standing beside his pack. Nicolas, his arm in a sling, solemnly promised not to stray away again. He had been assigned to watch over his mother and his sister.

Jeanne was still pale and out of sorts. Leaning against the

cabin door, she watched the departure scene. Her husband was going off with a light heart, knowing he was leaving behind a competent wife and happy children.

From the door, Jeanne waved at him one final time. She still felt his passionate kiss on her lips, a kiss that was meant for another. With relief she watched his tall figure recede, at the prow of one of the canoes. She could not stand to play the role of the strong and happy wife anymore, and gladly she looked forward to these weeks of solitude.

Perhaps a broken heart does mend in time, as a broken bone does. When the last canoe disappeared at the bend in the river, Jeanne closed the door and tried to convince herself she had been wishing for his departure, that it had become a necessity.

Her energetic nature quickly took the upper hand. Long periods of despair did not fit in with her optimism.

They settled down to a peaceful existence in the snow that fell the first night. Curled up in the big empty bed, Jeanne refused to think of Simon sleeping right on the frozen ground, somewhere in the forest. As long as he had not already met up again with the beautiful Indian woman who mends shirts with her hair.

During the months that followed, the mistress of the Rouville domain tried to better her and her family's lot in every possible way. Nicolas and Isabelle, grateful for their good fortune, came down to share her bed. Contrary to Simon's predictions, Gansagonas voluntarily abandoned her precarious shelter and moved into the loft. Only her brother Anonkade refused to live in the house.

When it was very cold, Mathurin was cordially invited to come sleep by the fire. He kept it going all night, which saved the mistress of the house a task.

As foreseen, Gansagonas became more and more open, won over by the king's daughter's warm friendship. Gansagonas turned out to be a very resourceful teacher. She taught the songs of her tribe and country recipes. In the evenings before the fire, the disparate groups listened with fascination to Jeanne's marvellous stories. The expert story-teller made mythology, ancient history and tales of chivalry live again.

On those occasions, even Anonkade came and sat on the ground near the door. He never spoke, but his sister assured Jeanne that he understood French very well.

As Pierre Boucher said in his book on Canada, "The winter, though the ground is covered with snow and the cold a bit harsh, is not always unpleasant. It's a cheerful cold."

When the temperature permitted, the group went out for some fresh air. Anonkade and Gansagonas fashioned snowshoes for everyone, including tiny Isabelle. They hardened the light wooden hoops in the fire and bent them into an oval shape, then crisscrossed them with thin strips of leather called "babiches." Fur-lined moccasins let them walk lightly and quickly. Muffled up to the eyes, Jeanne and the children learned how to snowshoe.

Carried away by Jeanne's enthusiasm, Anonkade fashioned a rough toboggan with two wooden planks raised at one end and fastened with straps.

Miraud was growing every day, much to Jeanne's dismay. The dog agreed to pull Nicolas and Isabelle in that unstable vehicle. The operation ended with tumbles in the snow and cries of delight. The three comrades, Jeanne and the children, also discovered the pleasure of sliding down the slope to the frozen river, all piled together on the fast-moving toboggan.

Jeanne had always been one to frolic. For weeks she had forced herself to be levelheaded in her husband's presence, and now her true nature rose to the surface. The more she laughed and sang, the more the children blossomed.

It was not until evening, in the silence of the night, punctuated only by Gansagonas's and Limp's snoring, that Jeanne would again feel the pain she had managed to dull during the day. A proud woman, she chased away these dark thoughts, refusing to cry over an ungrateful man who, when he thought of her, called her by another woman's name.

Jeanne often accompanied Mathurin as he dragged his foot through the snow to make the rounds of his traps. The old hunter soon noted with surprise that she knew almost as much as he did. Despite the frigid temperature, the habits of the animals of the Canadian forest were not so different from those of her grandfather's quarry. Even the traps were similar.

Soon she was able to make the rounds for him when the poor crippled man's rheumatism kept him home by the fire.

Several times before Simon had left, coureurs de bois or Indians had stopped their canoes to greet the lord. If the visitors brought along someone who was hurt or sick, which happened quite frequently, Jeanne's medical talents were put to use. She had learned Sister Bourgeoys's notebook by heart, and it enabled her to face every situation. The advice and herbs offered by the healers of Sorel and Chambly proved invaluable.

Little by little, the reputation of the "little Rouville lady" grew and spread. Several times during the winter, people arrived on snowshoes, coming to ask for advice or remedies for stubborn illnesses.

Always hospitable, Jeanne would add a hot meal to her detailed prescriptions. People even came to get her for desperate cases, taking her miles away to cabins hidden in the forest. Jeanne learned that she did have neighbours in New France—neighbours who lived five, ten or twenty miles away.

They escorted the healer or pulled her on a sled if the journey was too long. She was often absent for several days, but Limp and Gansagonas looked after the children. "In New France, you don't refuse very often. Everybody has to do his share," Carrot-Top had said.

With her practical spirit, Jeanne asked for payment in kind when people offered to reward her for her services. She was promised a pig and some chickens in the spring. Jeanne cared for an old lady's son who had gashed his foot with an axe, and the lady gave her some grey wool and taught her to knit. When she returned home, she awkwardly and laboriously knitted mittens for everyone, from Mathurin to Zeanne the doll.

She accumulated rare and sought-after potatoes and sacks of dried apples. She fell heir to a kitten who elected to live in Zeanne's cradle; its satisfied purring blended with that of the fire on the hearth. Miraud, as large as a wolf, patiently played the role of adoptive father to the tyrannical little feline.

Jeanne learned to deliver babies, set fractured bones and, unfortunately, wrap the dead.

One unforgettable night, a taciturn Huron took her on a mad dash to his village, eight miles from her house. In one of the longhouses where the Indians were gathered together in silence, they showed her a child, the son of one of the tribe's great chiefs. The boy was suffocating from an attack of false croup.

Jeanne remembered Old Hippolyte from Chambly telling her that many tribes had a custom of building "sweat rooms." The Indian people would shut themselves up in these sorts of ovens. Coming out of these bathhouses, they would jump into the river and give themselves a vigorous rubdown. Unfortunately, there was no sweat room in the longhouse, so Jeanne ordered the men to erect a tent made of blankets in the middle of the floor. Shut up in that shelter with the sick child in her arms, Jeanne had burning hot stones brought to her and cold water poured on them. The heavy steam helped the child breathe.

By morning the child was safe. Jeanne, exhausted and dripping with sweat, handed him back to his mother. Jeanne saw the gratitude in her eyes and considered herself rewarded.

Some time later, the Hurons returned for her to treat the hundred-year-old chief, who was asking nothing more than to go and join his ancestors. As she listened to the dying man, the poacher's granddaughter discovered that the Great Manitou's hunting grounds were very similar to those where her grandfather, Honoré Chatel, awaited her. It was easy for her to imagine the two worthy old men sitting together beside a stream, lying in wait for the celestial game. The idea warmed her heart.

As destiny decreed, the old chief died. The chief's grandson revered his grandfather, but had been waiting impatiently for his turn to govern. He gave Jeanne a wolfskin coat, so warm and comfortable that she was never cold again.

A delegation of Hurons brought her home, dressed in furs, seated on a sled pulled along at a good clip by warriors shod in snowshoes. For a moment she wished that Simon could see her. Her heart sank anew as she reminded herself that even then he would probably imagine Aimée instead of her. She resolutely banished her heart's instinctive wish to make her husband party to her slightest undertakings.

At Jeanne's instigation, Christmas was a joyous and boisterous holiday for all the members of a household that had never known such amenities. They exchanged gifts that they had laboriously made on the sly. The mistress of the house served a festive meal. Limp drank to excess and was overcome by emotion while telling Jeanne that she was just as good a woman as his late mother.

Gansagonas declared confidentially that no one had ever laughed or sung in the Rouville house before. The lord's first wife was always sad and the house silent.

In her bed, Jeanne thought bitterly that that fact had not stopped Simon from loving Aimée forever. If their future happiness depended on her own silence, then it wouldn't last for long.

26

MARCH brought milder weather. A few tardy snow showers attempted to bring back winter, but spring was in the air.

One morning the ice of the Richelieu settled with a loud crack. It was the famous "break-up." The river was always among the first to become navigable because of its boiling current.

Two days later, a long, piercing whistle announced Simon's arrival well before the canoes appeared around the bend in the river.

Miraud, who suspected all strangers, got his hackles up and sounded the alarm. The children jumped up and down on the shore. Limp waved his arms and shouted in his falsetto voice. Choking with emotion, Jeanne bounded towards the riverbank without even thinking of putting on her cape. Carried away by her impulsiveness, she had forgotten all reticence.

The sight of Simon's familiar figure and the resounding call of his strong voice quickened her blood. His pale eyes set in a thinner face sought her out, ignoring all else.

Leaving the heavily laden canoe to the Hurons who were paddling it, he jumped into the icy water and came closer, arms outstretched.

Nicolas and Isabelle did not doubt for a moment this accolade was for them. They rushed to him with squeals of delight. For the first time in his life, Simon was being received with a show of welcome. He knelt and clasped his children to his heart. Above their heads, he looked into his pretty wife's fresh, smiling face; her eyes were full of tenderness.

Immediately the familiar demon whispered in Jeanne's ear: "It's Aimée he's coming back for." An icy chill filled her and, without her realizing it, spread to her overly expressive face. A shiver travelled through her.

Simon leaped to his feet and encircled her with authoritarian arms. As always, he did not measure his strength and she suffocated in his embrace.

Reclaiming his rights, as if she had been unable to think for herself during his absence, he scolded, "You're not dressed for walking around in the snow. Let's go inside right now."

He did not want to be too demonstrative while his mocking comrades and the Indians with their politely impassive faces were looking on. He had not realized his impetuosity had already betrayed him.

Monsieur de Rouville left Mathurin and Carrot-Top to organize the unloading of his rare possessions and many bundles of furs, and he went up to the cabin, whose chimney was sending out a brave stream of smoke. A ray of sunlight made their unique and magnificent two-foot square window, the pride of the family, shine in all its glory.

Miraud at their heels, the four Rouvilles went into their house, and the door closed behind them. Two minutes later, it opened again and Simon was seen pushing Nicolas and

Isabelle outside; he had just given them a message as urgent as it was useless to pass on to Carrot-Top. Even Miraud and the cat found themselves ignominiously chased outside.

The plank that barricaded the door fell firmly into place. Alone at last, Simon turned to his wife and whirled her around in the narrow room. His exuberance always brought the walls that enclosed him dangerously near. Any house became too small when he walked in, carrying with him the forest and the wide open spaces.

"Jeanne, Jeanne," he murmured into her hair. She listened, untrusting, awaiting the error that would betray him. And yet how much she wanted to abandon herself and know happiness with no restrictions!

27

FOR two weeks a frenzy of activity had the cabin in an uproar. Monsieur de Rouville felled trees and enlarged his estate, aided by Mathurin and Carrot-Top.

Unfortunately, when the month of April rolled around, he would have to leave again for Katarakoui, near Lake Ontario, to help his friend Cavalier de la Salle construct a fort for Governor Frontenac. The Builder's reputation laid some heavy responsibilities on him.

Limp and the Carrot-Top from Amiens were happy to be together again, and all day long they squabbled in a friendly way.

"Our Carrot-Top has changed all of a sudden," Simon confided to his wife. "He stands up to everyone, gets into more fights than a wolverine and doesn't take orders from anyone but me anymore. He talks about you with an exasperating reverence. Since this winter he's been a new man. I don't know what's got into him.

"In all honesty," Simon concluded, "it makes life more difficult, but in my heart I'm happy for him. He was a good fellow, but too timid and self-effacing."

"What" had gotten into the boy was careful not to reveal her part in the emancipation of her husband's protégé. A simple liberating remark had accomplished what ten years of his boss's affectionate joking had not been able to: "The important thing Carrot-Top, is that you are here."

If only Jeanne could solve her own dilemma with one sentence!

Simon often spoke of his friend who was to come and join him for the voyage to Lake Katarakoui.

"De Preux is returning from a long expedition in the north with La Salle. The three of us have already been on several trips together."

Jeanne sensed the regret that rang through Simon's voice, despite his attempts to hide it. It is not easy to give up the intoxication of freedom; she knew something about that herself.

Suddenly he raised his head, abandoning the bench he was building. His wife had asked for it to replace the uncomfortable log on the doorstep.

"Now that I think about it, Jeanne, de Preux is one of your compatriots. He told me he comes from Troyes. Perhaps you know him?"

A son of the nobility, Simon seemed unable to conceive of the solitary existence of an outlaw's granddaughter or of an orphan locked away in a cloister. Patiently Jeanne explained her background again and concluded, "I don't know any family by that name. I lived a very sheltered existence. Nobody ever fought a duel over me."

Simon set to work again with a very busy look. His wife's tongue was dangerously sharp lately.

Limp and his young colleague shared the little hut by the water. Gansagonas returned to her rustic shelter and the children climbed up to their loft every evening. Existence resumed its course, as if the master's brief stays were the real slices of life and all the rest, the long months of absence, were simply interludes of waiting.

Jeanne asked Simon to build her an oven outside, since she had learned to make bread on one of her healing expeditions. Several of her "clients" had given her flour, more precious than gold.

Monsieur de Rouville greeted the tales of Jeanne's cures with a grain of salt. The image of the weak, resourceless woman was hard to shake off; his first marriage had conditioned him to believe in it.

So one night he accompanied Jeanne, "just to protect her," when she went off with two sinister-looking individuals. Their elderly father had had his leg crushed under a tree he was cutting down. They moved rapidly along the barely visible paths. Rouville, carrying Sister Bourgeoys's sack, could not get over seeing his wife, wearing moccasins, her musket over her shoulder, keeping up that rapid pace mile after mile.

The operation took place amidst a chorus of the victim's yells and his aged wife's wailings. As soon as Simon's strength was no longer needed to hold down the patient, he rushed outside, pale and vomiting. Jeanne remembered her own reaction on board ship when she first tended an injured man; she went outside to offer Simon encouragement and give her verdict.

"The poor old man won't walk straight, but at least he'll live."

Simon was angry at his own weakness.

"I didn't hesitate when I had to put Limp's bones back in place. But seeing you sewing with your white thread in all that massacre turned my stomach. You're so calm and reassuring. There've been plenty of times when I would have appreciated your care."

"Like when you got that cut on your back?"

Was her innocent question going to lead him to confess about that beautiful long-haired Indian woman?

Not at all suspicious, Simon nodded. "That time, among others. You would have had a gentler hand than Carrot-Top. He treated me by spreading gunpowder in the wound and burning it."

"Oh, and who repaired your shirt?"

"Gansagonas did when I returned. Did you notice how she did it? She sews with her hair."

Now Jeanne was ashamed of her suspicions. After a few hours' rest, the Rouvilles set out for home. Overflowing with gratitude, the injured man's family insisted on giving them a present. To Simon's great amusement, Jeanne asked the eldest boy, a blacksmith, to make her a door for her bread oven.

In the meantime, before he brought her this much-deserved gift, the blacksmith gave her a pair of tongs to add to the rudimentary instruments in her medical bag.

28

THE snow still covered the ground, but the warm April sun was melting more of it every day.

"It smells like spring," said Limp. And with delight Jeanne discovered that short magical season in New France, when the air is light, and winter and summer wage open war before the amazed eyes of those who know how to watch for it.

They tapped the maple trees, and the sap ran into the bark containers. Gansagonas and Jeanne boiled it for a long time on big fires tended by the men. When the liquid had evaporated in a scented steam, maple sugar remained. They would lay in a supply for the year.

The procedures were interrupted from time to time by the children and even the coureurs de bois who begged for the pleasure of tasting the toffee poured onto the snow and rolled on sticks. Gansagonas frowned at the waste of the raw material.

With a wooden spoon, Jeanne stirred the delicious mixture which would boil furiously until one-twentieth of its initial volume remained. Her cheeks were ablaze, her hair curled from the steam and the tip of her tongue stuck out in her concentration.

Simon watched her indulgently, then consulted Nicolas

in all seriousness.

"Look at your mother standing over her cauldron. I wonder if she's a witch or a fairy. What do you think?"

Without a moment's hesitation, Nicolas replied, "She's a witch. They're much more fun than fairies. They fly around on brooms like Mama's. They can cast spells."

"If you're talking about casting spells, you're right. Your mother is a witch."

With April came the buds and the bustling activity of the birds building their nests. Kneading dough on the table, Jeanne listened nostalgically to the joyful songs.

"They're looking forward to a summer together, and we're preparing for another separation."

Her hands white with precious flour, she was hoping the bread wouldn't be as heavy this time as it was the first time. After that failure, at the sight of her disappointment and impatience at having gone to so much trouble for nothing, her teasing husband had declared sententiously, "An oven door doesn't necessarily make good bread...and neither does the healer."

He took his leave diplomatically as she threw him a furious look followed by a vengeful remark. "Maybe your oven is defective."

That morning Simon was cutting wood as he whistled, heating the famous oven white-hot in readiness for baking. Suddenly jovial shouts and cries of welcome announced a visitor.

"We would have to have a visitor right now," thought Jeanne, striking the elastic dough with her fist. Two loaves of bread were finishing rising near the hearth.

The door slammed noisily against the wall. Simon

declared happily, "Jeanne, we have a guest."

A tall figure stopped on the threshold. Blue eyes met Jeanne's and she stood stock-still, her breath taken away.

Almost in spite of herself, she murmured, "Thierry. You're Thierry de Villebrand."

Perplexed, the man stared at her lengthily. In his memory he saw a child's face, then he, too, exclaimed, "It's the foolish little bird from Troyes."

They examined each other, still incredulous, and warm smiles spread over their faces.

A mocking voice intervened. "Is it necessary to introduce you?"

Jeanne held out her right hand covered in flour, while with her left she instinctively gripped the gold medal hanging around her neck.

De Preux, transfixed, kissed her outstretched hand. He turned to Simon. "You've married my foolish little bird with the mustard."

"Come now, be polite," scolded Rouville, frowning. The cavalier attitude of his friend, always so courteous, offended him, and he was ready to defend his wife's honour. Simon had been eager to introduce his new wife to his best friend. Now he had the feeling he was an intruder in this astonishing reunion.

Thierry de Villebrand and Jeanne Chatel, their hands clasped, gazed into each other's eyes without a word.

"Aren't you Count Villebrand?" Jeanne asked, baffled. "And what about your lovely chateau?"

"My oldest brother inherited the title and the estate. Younger sons often go far away to seek their fortunes and drop names that are too cumbersome."

What would Anne, Geneviève and Marie say about this unexpected twist in their favourite story? Jeanne wondered, laughing. Caught up in the trap of her own legend, she asked, "What happened to your white horse?"

"I replaced it with a bark canoe."

Very naturally, they sat down facing each other on either side of the table, the dough waiting before them.

Thierry asked a question that left Simon completely flabbergasted. "Do you still keep mustard in your pocket?"

"How are your eyes?" replied Jeanne with a lack of logic that left her husband feeling lost.

"I can't stand anything with mustard in it. Do you still have a chateau in an oak tree?"

Simon, his hands on his hips, exploded, "Enough. I've been listening to you two. You're speaking my language but I can't understand a thing you're saying. Are you going to explain your code to me or should I go back and chop more wood?"

His very limited patience was exhausted; he had had enough of being a stranger in his own house.

"The oven!" cried Jeanne, her practical nature coming to the fore. "Don't let it cool down. These loaves are ready to go in, and I'll finish off the rest."

She put the baking sheet with the two rounds of dough into Simon's hands and pushed him towards the door. He shot his friend an irritated glance and went out, grumbling, "I might as well be outside for all I'm contributing to the conversation."

They heard the oven door slam and his axe furiously attacking the poor innocent logs.

Jeanne kneaded her dough energetically as she chatted

with Thierry. Without their realizing it, the years spent thinking of each other had brought them closer together than the few hours they had actually shared.

The evening meal found the Rouvilles together around the table. Good humour reigned once more, thanks to the children's exuberant friendliness. Offering their guest a slice of bread that was still warm, the amateur baker remarked, "I'm returning the crust you gave me long ago."

They recounted the story of their youthful meetings to Simon. With her usual honesty, Jeanne told the fantastic tale she had spun. Her description of Thierry, as handsome as the statue of Saint Michael, still applied. The modest hero blushed, while his pitiless best friend roared with laughter.

The desperate courage of the orphan who had fought for her freedom had sustained Thierry through many of his ventures. The medal he had retrieved and given to her with so much delicacy of feeling glimmered softly, the symbol of their bond.

Simon watched the young, lively pair joking like childhood friends. He felt old, stern and taciturn. He was convinced that if de Preux had appeared at the church as planned the morning of their wedding, Jeanne would not have said "I do." Besides, had she not balked at pronouncing the fateful syllable, even in the absence of her handsome knight?

Monsieur de Rouville put on a preoccupied face to hide his distress. The preparations for his departure for Katarakoui demanded all his time. Too often he was forced to leave them alone together, two characters in a love story in which he had no part.

On the third morning after Thierry's arrival, the flotilla of canoes that belonged to the Fort Katarakoui builders stopped in front of the Rouville property.

The Builder was cheered and teased. Everyone greeted Captain de Preux in a friendly way; obviously he was a well-known and respected figure. This intrepid explorer, companion to Cavalier de la Salle, was planning new expeditions that would take him away again for several years.

He confided his ambitions to Jeanne. She shook her head.

"It's your way of finding the sailing ship of your youth. You're going off in search of your dreams."

"And you, Jeanne, you've found your chateau in the forest of New France. I couldn't wish for a more suitable companion for Simon. Until now he's known more pain than joy in his life."

"So I understand," said Jeanne, her face clouding over.

Aimée's pale ghost still floated between the couple. As for Simon, he was adding the more substantial one of Thierry on a white horse.

But when the time for leaving came, that did not keep Monsieur de Rouville from clinging to his wife like a drowning man grasping a floating plank.

The imprint of sadness was on Jeanne's face. Taciturn, Simon was sure that the seductive captain's departure was leaving her inconsolable, despite the happy farewells the two of them had exchanged.

At the cold expression in his pale eyes, Jeanne said to herself, He still hasn't forgiven me for not being his Aimée. Time doesn't heal anything. Quite the opposite. He'll never love me.

Rouville raised his paddle and gave the signal to depart. Long after the last canoe had disappeared, snatches of the voyageurs' song still hung in the air.

Tu as le coeur à rire,
Moi je l'ai-t-à pleurer.
Lui y a longtemps que je t'aime,
Jamais je ne t'oublierai.

"Come, children, we're going to get the ground ready to grow a garden. Nicolas will plant beans and Isabelle corn. We'll have to build a fence to stop Miraud from trampling the plants."

Life went on. From the very moment Simon left, Jeanne's period of waiting began, and she wanted to fill the time with a thousand different projects.

29

THE first tender shoots broke through the ground in the garden. Jeanne and the children, smeared with bear grease to keep off the blackflies, were waging war against the weeds. The cat and Zeanne, side by side, were sharing the cradle set in the sun.

Sitting at the foot of a tree, Gansagonas was fashioning a shirt and leggings for her mistress like those the coureurs de bois wore. Simon had brought back several deerskins, and Jeanne had requested this outfit to facilitate her comings and goings in the forest, on foot or on snowshoes. Having more than once travelled ten miles weighed down by a soaked skirt was enough to make her prefer comfort to convention.

Suddenly Miraud, hackles raised, burst into fierce barking.

"He smells a stranger," Nicolas announced.

Jeanne seized her musket leaning against the garden fence and ordered the children to run to the house. Regretting that Mathurin and Anonkade had gone off hunting, she was preparing to barricade herself inside when a call drowned out the dog's furious barking.

A long speech proclaimed in a female voice calmed Gansagonas, who was gathering up her work in haste. She announced, "Algonquins. They come see us."

These visits sometimes brought wandering bands into the little clearing. The Algonquins were freshly converted Christians who were often starving or ill. Charity dictated that a friendly welcome be given them. Besides, the one great principle of the colony had to be honoured. "You don't refuse very much in New France."

This time, five emaciated women dressed in rags came towards the cabin. Gansagonas went to meet them and act as interpreter.

Jeanne's heart ached to see such misery. She went into the house and returned with biscuits, raisins and the remains of some smoked eel.

The children came out of hiding, fascinated as always by the novelty of visitors. Nicolas, his wooden gun over his shoulder, put his hand on Miraud's head. The dog's constant growling made his body vibrate as if he were purring.

Isabelle, her long blonde hair cascading to her shoulders, was holding onto Jeanne's skirt and fiercely sucking her thumb. An Algonquin woman smiled broadly. She took hold of one of Isabelle's golden curls, then let go of it again.

In what could have been an expression of thanks, the emaciated women murmured a few soft words and went off into the forest, disappearing with the ease of people of their race. That night they would rejoin their nomadic band, and the next day they would continue their wanderings.

Two days later Nicolas received permission to accompany Mathurin when he went to set his traps. These two good friends—the cripple and the little boy—took Miraud with them; soon he would be made into an excellent hunting dog. Anonkade was visiting his tribe for the summer.

Gansagonas, her sack over her shoulder, went in search of ash tree bark from which she made poultices to treat Limp's rheumatism.

Jeanne took advantage of this welcome solitude to try an experiment that had been tempting her since the first warm days. She wanted to bathe and swim in the river. The current wasn't strong in front of the house, and the pure water presented an irresistible attraction.

Dressed in their white cotton shirts, Isabelle and the king's daughter slipped into the cool water, squealing with delight. A strong friendship bound them; for the little girl, this first dip in the river was a lovely sensation. Her adoptive mother washed her beautiful honey-coloured hair. Then, wrapping her snugly in the grey cape, she set her on the river bank where the sun would warm her. Zeanne was sleeping like a good doll in her gentle arms.

Jeanne took her turn diving into the water, remembering the strokes she had practised in the pond in Troyes. In long, lazy movements, she slid away from the bank. She floated on her back, rinsing her loose hair, cradled by the song of the birds and the murmur of the current. She admired the purity of the sky and felt happy despite the memory of that phantom woman. After all, she was strong, vibrant and passionate.

She turned towards the river bank and got her footing. The cape was spread out like a grey cloud, and Zeanne, abandoned, was lying on the sand. Isabelle had disappeared.

Intrigued at first, then displeased, Jeanne called and looked for her, growing more and more frantic. After an hour's search, Jeanne fired three shots, the distress signal that brought Gansagonas and the hunters hurrying back.

Miraud growled, prowling around the cape. After inspecting the area, Mathurin concluded, "Someone has kidnapped the little one."

Nicolas burst into sobs. Neither the old hunter nor the Huron woman could find any clear tracks.

Discouraged, Jeanne said, "It must be the Algonquin women we fed. One of them was admiring Isabelle. Where can we find them now?"

Gansagonas, still showing no emotion despite the disappearance of the child she adored, spoke in her language. By now Jeanne could understand her very well.

"Anonkade told me a group of nomads camps every summer east of here, near Sault aux Brochets. Perhaps those women are part of that group. I can go parley with them."

Jeanne sprang immediately into action, "I'm going with you, Gansagonas. Limp and Nicolas will stay here."

Unfortunately Mathurin could no longer undertake long expeditions; otherwise he would have already been on his way.

Gansagonas raised her hand. "My brother also told me those people detest palefaces because of a quarrel over hunting grounds. You'll be running a big risk by going to see them."

"If I don't go to see them, Gansagonas, I'll never be able to sleep in peace again."

This reasoning was enough to convince Gansagonas. The two women made their preparations for the journey immediately, and soon they had disappeared into the forest. Jeanne carried her musket, more out of habit than conviction. What good was one gun against a hostile tribe? She knew about the peace treaties the Algonquins had signed with the whites. But up to what point was a wandering band, obviously outside the law, restrained by the commitments made by its chiefs? They could very well do away with her, an intruder, then disappear themselves into the depths of the forest.

Sometimes the renegades would not hesitate to take trusting allies prisoner, only to trade them to the Iroquois for weapons or supplies. None of these considerations slowed Jeanne's determined pace. If there was one chance in a thousand of finding Isabelle, she had to take it.

The next day, after a few hours of rest taken in the pitch-black night, the two women reached the top of a hill. From there they overlooked a clearly temporary village of bark tents.

Despite her knowledge of the woods, Gansagonas had lost much time getting her bearings, since the Algonquins had changed their campsite.

No sentinel raised the alarm. Was the camp poorly guarded, or were visitors expected and already announced?

Gansagonas studied the Indians' comings and goings at length. Not one of the five women who had visited the Rouvilles was to be seen. Neither was there a little blonde girl in sight. Suddenly an Indian woman emerged from a shelter.

Gansagonas pointed at her. "That one came."

That was all the proof Jeanne needed.

Surrounded by four of his men, a chief was sitting in front of the biggest tent. With her guide Gansagonas, Jeanne had coolly discussed the best way to proceed as they walked through the forest. Her plan of action was set. Gansagonas silently withdrew and disappeared into the forest.

Jeanne leaned her useless musket against a tree and reached into her game sack. She took out the Spanish shawl, her most splendid ornament, and put it around her shoulders over the grey dress that had been mended at least a hundred times. Resolutely, she untied her long hair and let it spread over her back like a provocation. Then, with a firm step, she started down the hill, singing Simon's favourite tune in a strong, clear voice:

À la claire fontaine
M'en allant promener...

She walked between the rough tents without seeing them; they were but dancing images before her eyes. In the silence pulsating with sunlight, only her song rang out, like a challenge. Was that a muffled cry she had heard coming from one of the shelters?

Her head high, Jeanne de Rouville stopped in front of the chief, crossed her arms over her chest and waited calmly in silence.

Piercing eyes, their expression impenetrable, stared out at her coldly. With an imperceptible nod of his head, the Algonquin indicated she could speak.

Jeanne raised her hand as she had seen Simon do when he began a dialogue with the Indians. At the same time a quick prayer ran through her mind: "Grandfather, Mother Berthelet, François, ask God to give me inspiration."

First she questioned, "Does the great chief of the Algonquins speak my language?"

A sound that could have been interpreted in a thousand different ways was her answer. She boldly chose to believe it was an assent.

She went on, "A woman of your tribe had no daughter.

A woman of your tribe chose mine and tore her from my arms. Since then, that woman is happy, but my daughter and I have felt our hearts break. Could you in your wisdom allow a branch to be torn from a tree, then let both the tree and the branch die from it? I made my nest at the edge of the river. There I nurtured my young. One of them has been taken from me, and now the sun shines for me no more."

The words flowed, abundant and flowery, from her lips. She surprised herself with her own eloquence. Yet her listeners' impassive expressions filled her with doubt. Perhaps they did not understand a word she was saying. All her rhetoric might have been spent to absolutely no end. But what did it matter? Her firm voice and lively gestures kept them in suspense. If loquacity was needed to save Isabelle, then nothing would stop the flow of words from her mother. The storyteller plumbed her repertory for all the legends, all the situations in which parents have a joyful reunion with their lost children. No analogy with nature escaped her.

"Daughterly feelings, flesh of my flesh, comfort of my old age, star of my nights, fire that warms me—" she used them all. In one part of her mind the irrepressible Jeanne believed she could see her three protectors in Heaven engaged in quick consultations, spelling each other off to furnish her with ideas. She sprinkled her speech with songs, sayings and bit of poetry.

The sun was setting, and the chill of the evening made her shiver. Her lips were dry and her throat tight. Fires had been lit, but she did not dare turn her head to inspect the camp. Her eyes did not leave those of the Algonquin chief.

Vaguely she felt a circle of spectators form around her. For five hours her voice did not falter and her trembling legs miraculously supported her. She recited a poem she had learned in the orphanage that had surfaced from deep in her unconscious:

There is nothing sweeter, nothing sweeter
than a mother,
But for, but for her child.

Abruptly Jeanne fell silent, unable to say another word. With her flair for drama, she took the colourful shawl from her shoulders. Stretching out her arms, she let it fall at the chief's feet, where it lay in a shimmering pile like an offering of light.

Dressed in grey, her head bare, her hands open before her, she waited. She had given all the courage and love she possessed; she had no more left.

A lengthy silence held sway over the gathering. You would have to know the Indians' soul to understand the extraordinary effect of the spectacle they had just witnessed. Even those who did not understand French had followed the drama.

The chief raised his hand and gave an order, looking over Jeanne's shoulder. As she turned around slowly, the circle of Algonquins opened to make room for a skinny woman who was leading Isabelle by the hand.

Without a word, the mother and the daughter reached out and held each other in an embrace only death could break.

The woman who had stolen the child stood motionless. At a signal from the chief, she seized the beautiful shawl meant for an unknown fiancée. François from on high

176

could hardly blame his benefactress.

Clutching the trembling child to her breast, the "little Rouville lady" walked through the village, looking neither to the right nor to the left. In a joyful voice she sang her war song:

Sur la plus haute branche
Le rossignol chantait...

She squeezed Isabelle in her arms, and the child added her frail little out-of-tune voice to her mother's. The entire village watched silently as they slowly climbed the hill. Soon the sound of the French song faded into the night.

No one followed them. Gansagonas loomed like a shadow from the trees. She was carrying the musket and the game sack, and preceded them through the dark forest.

Jeanne moved like a sleepwalker, suffocating the little girl in an embrace worthy of Simon. Tears of tension and fatigue rolled down her cheeks.

"Why are you crying, Mama? Aren't you happy to see me?" Isabelle asked timidly.

Jeanne kissed her blonde head fervently. With a gentle laugh she explained, "I'm crying out of happiness. Later on you'll discover that crying is the greatest sign of happiness."

30

A FAMILIAR whistle pierced the silence. Jeanne put down the basket of beans she was picking and ran towards the river. Her heart was pounding and, as in the past, she pressed both hands to her chest.

A canoe was approaching, and a friendly arm waved a paddle. A stentorian voice set the echoes rolling.

"Hey, Rouville, I've got some news!"

In one agile movement, the voyageur stopped his canoe near the river bank. He had a magnificent reddish-brown beard. Jeanne recognized Charron the trapper, her old paddling teacher.

"Bonjour, monsieur. My husband isn't here. He's spending the summer at Katarakoui. But you're welcome anyway."

"Greetings, little lady. Rouville isn't here? That's unfortunate. He's running the risk of having what he'd call 'misunderstandings' if he doesn't go to Ville-Marie as soon as possible."

While his hostess served him a meal of cold meat and strawberry pie, Charron explained the situation.

Frontenac had just issued an edict requiring all trappers to obtain permits to trade in furs. The governor was afraid of smuggling and illegal dealings. He was attempting to protect his interests and those of France, if not those of the settlers.

"Perrot, the governor of Montreal, has to send the list of applications to Quebec by the end of the month. If Rouville doesn't sign up, he'll lose all his rights. And since Perrot and he often have...'misunderstandings' about the governor's fraudulent little dealings with the Indians...well! He'll have a good opportunity to settle a grudge."

Jeanne was shattered. She knew that despite his resolutions to cultivate the land, Simon was above all a man of the woods. Besides, after his forced absence during the summer, only another winter of taking furs would enable him to build up his pocketbook again.

For an hour she questioned her talkative visitor. His belly full, flattered by the attention she gave his every word, the good trapper provided her with all the information she needed.

Towards the end of the afternoon, he left with the Indian who was escorting him. He said he would be paddling up to Lake Champlain, and would come back via the Rouvilles' when he returned in six days.

"I'm supposed to go up to Ville-Marie with a group of fellows who are applying for permits. I'm making the rounds to let them know, since the decision was so sudden. The governor is going to catch a lot of them by surprise."

François-Marie Perrot, disliked by the coureurs de bois because of his arrogance and dishonesty, was going to take advantage of the edict to get his revenge on some of them.

"Don't forget to stop for a meal on the way back," urged Jeanne, in keeping with the rules of hospitality.

"Simon's damned lucky," muttered the trapper as he

waved goodbye to her.

Six days later, faithful to their meeting, Charron paddled swiftly towards the shore. Unceremoniously, he had invited his friends to share in the invitation. Seven canoes containing ten hunters and four Hurons advanced upon the little beach.

No smoke came from the chimney. The precious window was boarded up and the door closed. Immediately on the alert, the voyageurs grabbed their guns.

A clear voice hailed them from the forest and a boy appeared, musket in hand, a sack over his shoulder.

"Hey, Charron! The Rouvilles have gone to visit the Bibeaus who are marrying off their daughter. My sister asked me to apologize for her."

"Your sister?" asked Charron, looking over the slender boy from head to foot. As he was, the boy was dressed in a fringed suit, and his short brown hair was sticking out from under an enormous fur cap. His grey eyes stared right back at the trapper as he inspected him.

"You do resemble her...but you're not as pretty."

Briskly, the young man continued, "I'm Jean Chatel. And I'd like to go down to Ville-Marie with you."

Curious, the voyageurs came closer. Some of them dug into their pockets and pulled out some pemmican, since the invitation to dinner was no longer forthcoming.

Charron spit, scratched his reddish-brown beard and asked, "What do you want to do in Ville-Marie?"

"Sign a trading contract, of course," came the insolent voice.

A general outburst of laughter greeted this statement. Gibes were heard from all sides.

180

"If babies start at it, there's going to be a shortage of game."

"You have to have a beard to get a permit. It's one of Frontenac's rules."

"How old are you, Junior?" Charron asked the disappointed young Chatel.

The boy stood up straight again. "Thirteen. Soon I'll be fourteen. I can paddle and set traps. I won't get in your way."

"Good, then get in. And to prove your usefulness, you're the one who's going to soak your moccasins pushing the canoes into the water."

Amid laughter and rough jokes, poor Jean, sweating and red in the face, braced himself with all his might to launch the bark boats one by one into the water. The soft sand at that spot in the river allowed the voyageurs to beach the canoes without any danger of staving in the bottoms.

Sitting in the centre of the canoe paddled by Charron and a Huron, the boy, soaked to his thighs, caught his breath and watched the Rouville house disappear around the bend in the river.

If Simon could see me now, thought Jeanne, taking off the fur cap she'd borrowed from Nicolas. Despite the heat, every man wore one, almost as a symbol of his profession. She shook out her short hair and felt the bite of the sun and the mosquitoes on her bare neck.

After all, perhaps it was better if her husband did not see her. That way he would retain a few illusions about the femininity of the king's daughter he had fallen heir to.

For the first time in her life, Jeanne felt as if she were on holiday. The children were safe at the Bibeaus' house with

Limp and Gansagonas. She had told everyone she had to miss the wedding to help deliver a baby. Returning home alone, she had proceeded with her transformation. Her beautiful brown hair, sacrificed for a good cause, was hidden in her trousseau chest.

The suit Gansagonas had made her was very comfortable; the tight binding squeezing her proud bosom was much less so. By taking off the belt she wore low on her hips, she could spare herself the torture, since the shirt hung loosely around her.

By the time I get to Ville-Marie I'll be bent over for good, especially if I have to keep my shoulders hunched even when I'm paddling.

Meanwhile, the river sparkled like a pathway of diamonds, and the echo of that joyful song rang out:

À la claire fontaine
M'en allant promener...

Suddenly she felt herself blushing to the roots of her hair. The couplet that the paddlers were noisily singing was much naughtier and racier than any she had heard before.

Jeanne chuckled to herself. That was only the first of the problems her escapade would present. Charron would have certainly agreed to take Madame de Rouville along, but the presence of a woman would have embarrassed the other coureurs de bois, most of them misogynists. All the same, she felt that Carrot-Top and Limp accepted her. All at once, the truth came to her.

A wife accompanied by her husband was not a real person, but just a pale reflection, a creature without substance who existed only because someone had given her his name. For these rough men, a woman anywhere else but in her house was a burden, an unnecessary risk, an inevitable responsibility.

Her eyes full of fire, the little Rouville lady swore that very instant never again to play that self-effacing role. Too bad for Simon and his restrictive illusions, and the devil with the timid, submissive and sweetly transparent wife. Jeanne Chatel would be recognized for what she was or sent back, bag and baggage, to the king.

In the meantime, the audacious Jean Chatel, the boy who was accompanying the coureurs de bois, quickly discovered that strength alone made the laws in this primitive society.

"Jean, go find some wood."

"Junior, bring some water."

"Hey, Junior! Bring some more water, you shirker."

Very much in demand from all sides, Junior, dead tired and furious, became everybody's servant. They made him pay dearly for the favour of travelling with the men. It was the whole story of the overly submissive Carrot-Top all over again.

Jeanne was quite determined not to give these hard men any reason to justify their opinions about weak women. At every stop she went right to work. She was spared some tasks, thanks to tricks inspired by her indignation.

The first evening, after forcing her to gather the makings, they gave her the responsibility of building the fire. Unaccustomed to that type of chore, she smoked up the entire camp by burning green branches on purpose. She was then relieved of that responsibility. Charron gave her an old hunting knife and handed her the partridges to clean and pluck. Then he put her in charge of watching the pot in which the fowl she had prepared were simmering. All this time, the lazy men were lounging around, shouting instructions at her.

They take me for a slave, she thought spitefully.

She let the supper burn and got off with eating pemmican and spending an hour cleaning the charred disaster off the bottom of the pot. They never gave her that job again.

Later that evening, on the pretext that she needed a lot of sleep, she slipped under Charron's canoe and went to sleep, rolled up in an old blanket that Simon had abandoned. That way she avoided the coarse campfire jokes that had Junior as their butt.

Curious in spite of it all, she lent an ear to the tales of the coureurs de bois. She found that these rough men respected Simon for his experience, authority and great bravery.

Charron, the indiscreet gossip, had guessed that Monsieur de Rouville's first wife had been more of an ordeal than a consolation, always afraid, tearful and dissatisfied.

"Now, take the new one, for example. There's a capable woman for you. She can handle a frying pan and a paddle like no one else."

While the heroine, her cheeks aflame, hid under her blanket, everyone laughed loudly over the adventure at Quatre-Ruisseaux.

A Huron, usually not very talkative, asked to speak. He told the lengthy story of how Isabelle had been saved, which he had heard from an Algonquin friend.

"From noon until sunset, the words of that white woman flowed like honey into the Algonquins' ears."

The young mother's audacity and courage were much

appreciated. A joker who couldn't resist getting in his two cents said, "A woman who can go on for five hours at a time, that would scare me a little."

"Rouville won't always have the last word," Charron concluded as he spat into the fire.

A smile on his lips, Jean Chatel fell asleep, taking no notice of the fine rain that was beginning to fall.

At Fort Chambly Hubert de Bretonville came down to the dock to meet the voyageurs. The junior of the group, his head turned towards the river, carefully avoided attracting attention. Charron and the two others accepted the captain's invitation to dine with him.

Jeanne slipped over to see her old friend, Hippolyte. She had several specific questions to ask the healer. She introduced herself as Jean Chatel, the brother of Madame de Rouville. Faced with the skepticism she read in his discerning eyes, she admitted her trickery. She slept on dry ground right by the fireplace, on a straw mattress her host had given her. She left the next day with fresh supplies of medicine and advice.

At Ville-Marie the crafty boy played his role with confidence. Thanks to childhood memories, Professor Limp's lessons and the information he had pried from Charron and the unsuspecting trappers, he correctly answered the agent's questions concerning the quality of the fur skins, the types of traps and the demarcation of the hunting territory. Having proved his competence despite his young age in that land where children were considered men, he obtained fur trading permits in the name of his "brother-in-law," Simon de Rouville, and in his own name. With a firm hand, Jeanne signed "J. Chatel" and put down the required

185

guaranty. Through a doorway she caught sight of Governor Perrot watching the transactions. She repressed a strong desire to stick out her tongue at him in triumph.

Finally, her contract safely in her pocket, she wandered like a sightseer through the streets of the town. She had declined her travelling companions' friendly invitation to accompany them to the inn for a celebration.

She didn't push her audacity as far as going to visit Sister Bourgeoys. Simon would have been the first to suffer from the gossip caused by her masculine attire and short hair. It took very little to provoke a scandal in the puritan colony.

At nightfall a timid, polite young boy asked for shelter at the Hotel-Dieu. The Mother Superior of the hospital let him sleep in a corner of the kitchen, after having made him bring in a good provision of wood. A practical person, she firmly believed that one good turn deserved another.

Jeanne had hoped to meet Mademoiselle Mance, the faithful friend whose merits Sister Bourgeoys had praised, and the founder of the first hospital in Ville-Marie. Unfortunately, this saintly woman had died the previous month, to the great regret of the entire colony that worshipped her. Jeanne was surprised to see how unmarried women like Marguerite Bourgeoys and Jeanne Mance had succeeded in asserting themselves through their personal value, whereas married women seemed eternally destined to live in the shadow of their worthy husbands. She would have liked to know Simon's opinion on that subject. How would he accept his young wife's new spirit of emancipation?

He'll just have to get used to it, Jeanne decided resolutely. From now on she wasn't playing any more roles. A fool-

186

ish laugh came over her when she realized she was making those laudable resolutions at the very moment she was sleeping in front of the hospital fireplace, disguised as a boy by the name of Jean Chatel.

The next morning, most of the trappers left for their preferred hunting grounds. Charron had lost the Huron who continued on to Quebec. He asked his young friend to paddle in his place at the front of the canoe.

For two hours she kept up the exhausting rhythm before admitting defeat. They were alone in their boat, far behind the others because of the second paddler's weakness.

Charron spat into the water, cleared his throat and grumbled, "Lie down in the bottom of the boat, little lady. I'm going to take you home without tiring you out. You certainly deserve it."

"What? You knew?" asked Jeanne, astonished.

"I recognized the way I taught you to paddle. You really took us in, the fellows and me. Nobody suspected a thing."

Blushing and suddenly embarrassed, the trapper remembered certain stories and several very risqué songs. Jeanne reassured him with a laugh. She was a solid king's daughter, not a delicate, fragile lady. Nothing had shocked her; everything had interested her. The spirit of comradeship had touched her most of all.

"When Simon tells me about his journeys now, I'll understand what he's talking about."

"Damned Rouville," Charron said admiringly. "He has a one-in-a-million wife. That's just like him!"

Resting her painful shoulders on her pack at the bottom of the canoe, Jeanne couldn't help noticing the trapper's typically masculine attitude. He still managed to give his

187

companion all the credit for finding himself an exceptional wife.

Out of habit, Jeanne lifted her hand to her neck, but her gold medal wasn't there. She had given it to Perrot's agent as a guaranty for the trading permit. Grandfather would understand her sacrifice, just as François had. Light-hearted, her soul at peace, Jeanne de Rouville was on her way back to her lord's domain.

That evening in the camp, poor Charron, obliged to play a role as well, experienced the entire range of emotions. He was so indignant at the abuses of his comrades who were making Junior work that he forgot his own recent demands. He changed the subject of conversation by noisy awkward interruptions when they approached areas that were too risqué. With a deafening whistle he drowned out the words to the songs Jeanne now knew by heart. His exasperated friends gave him a tongue-lashing, and his very amused passenger did her best to put him at ease.

A few months later, Jeanne learned that at first Charron had no intention of going farther than Sorel, where he had a hunting contract for the fort.

Using the pretext of an urgent meeting at the river's source, he continued the journey until his young companion, Jean Chatel, found himself at the Rouville property. Only then did he retrace his steps. Once he knew Jeanne's secret, he would not have forgiven himself for not taking her back safely.

In the distance, hidden among the trees, he watched the boy enter the deserted cabin. An hour later, out came Madame de Rouville, modestly dressed in grey, her black scarf tied around her short hair.

In her long hunter's stride, Jeanne headed for the Bibeaus' house, twelve miles away. Her lack of experience in the forest kept her from suspecting that, a hundred steps behind her, followed a devoted and discreet protector. Charron breathed easily only when he saw Jeanne holding her children in her arms and getting ready to take them back under Limp's watchful eye.

Limp scrutinized the forest at length, suspicious, a frown on his face. His instinct had warned him of something unusual in the air. When he went ahead to investigate, Charron was already far away, running to his canoe and hurrying towards Sorel to fulfill his obligations and furnish the garrison with game for the coming months.

31

THE ears of Indian corn, soon to be harvested, waved in the summer breeze. As she did every afternoon when she could get away, Jeanne had taken refuge at the top of the old oak and was scanning the river. One day she would spot a canoe with a familiar figure in the front. The Builder would be returning home and life would begin anew.

A vibration in the tree pulled her from her thoughts. Light cracking noises signalled the approach of a climber who was as silent and agile as a cat.

Was it an enemy? Her musket, hanging lower down at the fork, was out of reach. Jeanne took her knife in her hand and waited, trembling in her nest of rustling greenery.

The leaves shook and parted. A brown hand closed over her ankle above her moccasin. Dressed in Jean Chatel's favourite attire, she straddled a solid branch, well braced against the trunk. She raised her weapon, ready to sell her life dearly.

A black head of hair appeared at her feet. An astonished face turned upward, and pale eyes stared at her in disbelief.

"Simon." She breathed a sigh of relief as her taut nerves relaxed. Louder, she repeated, "Simon" and finally all her joy broke through in one triumphant cry: "Simon!"

"Do king's daughters grow on trees now?" asked the

Builder in a husky voice.

In one supple movement he hoisted himself up and sat astride the same branch, facing her. With one hand he leaned against the trunk above her shoulder; with the other he caressed her short curly hair. His bantering voice was no match for the tenderness of his green eyes as he drank her in.

"Are you really my brother-in-law, Jean Chatel?"

"Oh, Simon! You're back! If you only knew..."

Imperious lips interrupted her words. All the birds in the forest were singing in Jeanne's ears. If the overly strong grip he had on her brown curls had not held her back, she was sure she would have taken flight. More likely she would have tumbled from her perch.

Simon leaned back a few inches to look at his young wife's happy, tanned face, as if to rediscover its every feature. Only then did he ask the logical question. "What are you doing up here?"

"I was waiting for you. I was going to watch you arriving down there on the river one of these days."

"Never trust a husband. I took a short cut through the woods to get here faster."

"If you were running so fast, why did you climb the tree?"

"Because I do every time I go by. Remember, I told you. It's my observation post."

"Did you build your fort?"

"Yes. But at the last minute I handed it over to Frontenac and came home. I strongly advised him not to make any more plans involving me."

Another kiss interrupted the conversation. When Simon

looked at her again, she was splitting her sides laughing. His hackles raised, the lord frowned. Jeanne pressed her hands against his chest.

"How many daughters do you think the king has who get kissed at the top of an oak tree?"

"There's only one, and that's already one too many. You're going to split your head open on the way down. I'll help you."

The commanding voice already indicated the master had returned. Slipping out of his embrace, Jeanne put her leg over the branch, encircled the trunk of the oak and began a rapid and expert descent.

She retrieved her musket at the large fork while Simon, offended, swept past her. He jumped to the ground and held out his arms. He was convinced she couldn't do anything without his help...when he was there.

Willingly, she let herself drop into his comforting embrace. It was quite a while before Simon remembered to put her down on the ground. When he finally decided to do so, he sat down next to his pack and pulled her down beside him.

Sitting very close together, her curly head pressed against her beloved's chest, Jeanne said to herself that she had finally found happiness. For a long time they did not stir. Suddenly Simon rummaged in his shirt pocket, then dangled a gold chain with a shiny medal on it from the tip of his long fingers.

"Your brother forgot this in Ville-Marie. I got it back for you."

"Like Thierry did before."

Jeanne bit her tongue. It had been a spontaneous, involuntary remark, like Simon's cry when he called her Aimée. She waited, frozen with apprehension.

But Rouville laughed happily as he pulled her closer.

"That damned captain, 'as handsome as Saint Michael,' sends you his affectionate greetings. It seems that you're some sort of Joan of Arc to him. He's put you on a pedestal. That doesn't suit you at all. Your place is here on the ground with a humble mortal like me."

He kissed her again, stretched out his long legs and said, "Tell me about your summer. Now that we're partners in the fur trade, we shouldn't keep anything from each other."

"You already know about all that?"

"I stopped in Ville-Marie, thinking I'd lost my chance. To my great pleasure, I found my little brother-in-law had taken care of everything."

Simon was not a demonstrative man. He squeezed her a little tighter. That took the place of all the words of gratitude, but it was more than enough for her.

"Don't forget your epic adventure with the Algonquins. Don't hide anything from me because I know all about it."

"Oh? So you were having me watched?"

"You will discover, little Madame de Rouville, that our vast, wild country is as rife with gossip as the salons of your venerable father, Louis XIV."

"Who told you all my secrets?"

"Another of your passionate admirers. Charron was waiting for me at Sorel to sing me your praises." With an air of satisfaction he added, "He thinks I'm very clever to have found a wife like you. I am, in fact."

Jeanne sniffed disdainfully. Was there no limit to men's pretentiousness? Stung, she objected, "If you know everything, why make me talk about it?"

"Because I like you. And what interests me the most is your own version of your little escapades."

She closed her eyes lazily, feeling his voice reverberating behind her; every one of its sharp tones filled her with comfort. She felt relaxation come over her, and would have been quite surprised to discover that, of her own free will, she was falling into the very trap she wished to avoid: the trap of blissful dependence.

Pitiless, Simon gave her a shake. "Come on, talk. If you can chatter on for five hours for an Algonquin, you can certainly do the same for your husband."

The modest heroine talked at length of her solitude and her adventures. Her account was interrupted so often it threatened to last forever.

Running ahead of Gansagonas, Nicolas and Isabelle came looking for Jeanne. They discovered their parents at the foot of the oak, laughing and chatting, their arms around each other.

"Papa!" Isabelle cried enthusiastically.

Nicolas, more discerning, gave them a long look, his eyes so like his father's.

"Are you glad to see us again?" Needing to confide, he added, "You know, Papa, Mama borrowed my fur cap. And she put her hair away in her trunk."

32

A WEEK after Simon returned, Jeanne was picking the last raspberries in a little clearing. Nicolas and Isabelle were helping her, eating two berries for each one they put in the pot.

Miraud sniffed the air and growled; his fur stood on end. Jeanne put her hand firmly around his muzzle and silenced the animal.

Suddenly she sensed that she was surrounded. She could fire a shot to call Simon and Mathurin who were cutting wood near the house. This signal would alert the enemy at the same time and start a race between the two groups. At stake was her life and, most of all, that of her children.

Without letting go of the dog that was trembling with anger, Jeanne whispered an order. "Children, hide here in this bush and don't move. When the Indians are gone, Nicolas will count to ten two times, then take Isabelle by the hand and run to the house. Do you understand, Nicolas?"

"Yes, Mama," the child answered in a low voice.

Though his enormous eyes were filled with terror, his voice was steady.

"After you warn Papa, hide in the house. Quickly. Go inside and don't move. Even if you hear me yell, you must not come out until the last Indian has gone."

The branches closed over the crouching children. Jeanne replaced the leaves and rubbed out the footprints with her hand.

As tense as a deer on the alert, she waited. At her side the dog broke loose. A voice called out. The Indians must have been very sure of themselves to dare speak, they who usually glided as noiseless as shadows.

They appeared at the other end of the clearing between her and the house, blocking her escape route. There were four or five of them, and their headdress, which Mathurin had described a hundred times, proved they were Iroquois. They seemed unfamiliar with the territory; they glanced around as they talked quietly among themselves. Not for a second did Jeanne think of hiding. The Indians' piercing eyes would have quickly discovered her, and a search party would ensue that would turn up her two children.

Motionless, she blended in with the foliage. In spite of that, one of the Indians pointed her out. Now was the moment to act. With a cry of terror, Jeanne pretended to panic and turned circles, imitating the mother partridge's trick. Then she picked up her skirt and scurried off into the forest calling Miraud, who followed her against his will.

As she had planned, the Iroquois took off running and went past the children without seeing them. The way was clear for them to take refuge in the house.

The children were saved; now it was time to save the mother. Jeanne devoted herself fervently to doing just that. To encourage her pursuers, she kicked up an awful row. Then, saving her breath, she ran with long strides, cursing her burdensome skirt. She released the dog who turned around and faced the Iroquois, granting her a few seconds' respite. She took advantage of it to fire a shot into the air to alert Simon. She hated to waste her only bullet, but there was no time to turn around and aim.

The dog had fallen silent. Was he dead? Footsteps pounded behind her. There she stood at the ravine Nicolas had plunged into. Her desperate plan had led her there, as if that abyss could offer her safety.

She jumped between two bushes, threw herself on the ground, rolled on her stomach and, without a backward glance, let herself slide down the steep slope. This time she didn't try to slow her pace, and the stones that tumbled down and accompanied her descent didn't stop her any more than did the brambles that caught her dress.

Above, her pursuers were momentarily confused by her disappearance. They were in enemy territory. The woman had sounded the alarm. Was it worth the risk of following her into the ravine?

The sound of breaking branches, then shouts growing nearer, announced that help was on the way. A lone Indian let himself slide down after Jeanne. Less hurried than she was, he broke his fall and studied the way down.

Once he reached the bottom he turned around slowly, searching the hard stones and the tangle of dead trees for traces of his victim's path.

Up above, Simon had wings. Alerted by the shot, he picked up his gun without dropping his axe and bounded through the forest. Limp, forgetting his infirmity, was right behind him. Rouville met the children on their way back to the house; panic was on their faces, but he didn't slow his pace. Gansagonas would intercept them and take them back to safety. It was Jeanne he had to find. He, too, fired a shot into the air to tell her he was coming.

The alarm signal had come from the north. In that direction the path bordered the ravine. With unfailing instinct he hurtled along, leaping obstacles, making as much noise as possible and letting out his death cry, his specialty when he attacked. It always helped to rattle his enemies.

The last Iroquois wheeled around and waited for the assault. With a sudden turn Simon dodged him, leaving him to Mathurin who was coming along more slowly but making just as much noise.

Rouville stepped over the struggling forms of an Indian and Miraud. Near the ravine two of the enemy stood side by side to face the unleashed fury of Simon de Rouville in combat.

He hit one Indian over the head with the butt of his long musket, sending him toppling into the void with a loud scream. The other Iroquois threw himself on Simon, who had jumped aside so his momentum wouldn't send him into the ravine.

A gunshot behind him proved that Limp and his Iroquois had finally met. Simon and his foe rolled on the ground a few inches from the abyss. Each one was trying to send the other over the edge. The two fighters dropped both tomahawk and axe, useless in hand-to-hand combat. The thought of Jeanne gave Simon new strength. His forearm, pressed against his adversary's throat, was slowly choking him. The Indian was trying to push back Simon's head with his palm. His right hand, caught in Simon's iron grip, was nailed to the ground.

Limp burst onto the battlefield, hopping on one foot, using his musket as a crutch. He was out of breath but still full of spirit. He pulled his knife and limped forward. It had been a few years since he had taken part in a fight, despite his bellicose spirit. Simon and he were old comrades-in-arms and fellow adventurers, and they had shared many dangers together. They understood each other with scarcely a word being spoken.

"Leave this one to me," Mathurin said, panting. He raised his dagger over the Indian who was temporarily stunned by the pressure on his neck.

Without a word, Simon released his man. He rolled aside and let himself slide into the ravine as quickly and recklessly as his wife had a short time before.

At the bottom, he called "Jeanne" once, briefly, then he listened.

Near her hide-out, Jeanne had heard the loud and horrible fall of the body tumbling from above. Already her pursuer had reached the bottom of the ravine. Cowering under the tall tree where she had spent a night with Nicolas, she lay low, holding her quick breath and praying Simon would arrive before the Indian found her. Her only weapon was a dead branch, since her musket and knife had disappeared in her tumble.

She spotted the man's legs. He was searching for her systematically, without a word; only his panting breath gave him away.

Jeanne had heard Simon's call but did not dare raise her voice. The Iroquois stood between them, knife in hand. She retreated another inch and, crouching at the bottom of the hole, she waited. No sound reached her ears. She had the feeling this senseless adventure was all a dream, that the sun could never shine on such horror. Was this the same panic the mother partridge felt last summer when she turned circles to lead her enemies away from her endangered babies?

Jeanne, who had borrowed the mother partridge's trick, would have liked to ask her for her courage as well. She clapped her hand over her mouth to stifle a scream of terror. The branches parted. Her breath caught in her throat as a triumphant face with implacable eyes loomed before her.

Despite the stick she was waving, the Iroquois grabbed her wrist and twisted it, making her drop her club. In one sudden movement that propelled her to her enemy's feet, Jeanne felt herself being pulled from her hiding-place.

"Simon!" she finally cried, recovering the faculty of speech too late.

She was filled with rage at the thought of dying so stupidly just when she had found happiness, when the sky was so radiant. The friendly sun glanced gaily off the blade raised over the king's daughter, who was fighting like a wild beast, biting, spitting, swearing. Her hair in her eyes, she struggled for all she was worth. Her enemy gave ground, then again the hand grabbed her and shook her. All claws out, she managed to clamp her teeth onto a wrist. She did not hear the voice that was calling her. A resounding slap that sent her breathless to the ground brought her back to reality.

Simon was on his knees in front of her, straddling the body of the Iroquois.

He gasped, "My God, your teeth are sharper than a wolf's. And where did you learn that language?"

Blood was flowing from his wrist, but little by little a

200

dazzling smile spread across his tense features. He had just remembered that he and his trapper friends had been his gentle wife's professors of profane eloquence. The student was no lady, thank goodness. Who needed a woman who put on airs in the forest?

Weak and defenceless *after* the danger, Jeanne let herself be carried in his familiar arms. Man and wife were both literally in tatters, their clothes torn and their arms and legs skinned.

This time the climb was slow and painful. Mathurin was waiting for them at the top, furious with himself. At the last moment, his Iroquois had slipped between his fingers.

The one Miraud had intercepted so effectively was not to be found either. His flight was marked by bloodstains.

The big dog, his shoulder gashed by a tomahawk, agreed to be treated by Jeanne. She gave him a grateful kiss on the forehead.

The two seasoned coureurs de bois studied the fallen Iroquois and came to the conclusion it was probably an isolated group of young braves. Impatient at not being able to prove their valour in official raids, they had smeared themselves with war paint and ventured into the territory at the most dangerous time for them, when the hunters were working their fields and could defend their families.

It was safe to say that this was an isolated attack, not likely to be repeated. Just to be sure, Simon sent for Anonkade and another Huron, and he entrusted them with the safety of his family for the winter.

33

THE canoe glided silently between two walls of flaming trees. Once again, October was celebrating its passage with an orgy of fantastic colours.

Sitting in the bottom of the boat between two close-mouthed Indians, Jeanne compared this present voyage with last year's. At that time she hardly knew Monsieur de Rouville and had studied him with mistrust. Now she knew him, loved him and was flying to his rescue.

Simon, her Simon, was somewhere in the forest, seriously wounded. The Hurons with whom he hunted had come to fetch the healer. Carrot-Top had sent them, while he stayed with his leader. It was impossible to drag any information out of these Indians of Algonquin origin, whose dialect she couldn't understand.

They had come forth like shadows, conferred with Anonkade and waited patiently while their passenger assembled some clothes, blankets, her medicine bag and her two remaining cotton petticoats.

Nicolas loaned his cap again.

Dressed as a boy, draped in her cape and carrying her wolfskin coat, Jeanne took her place in the canoe without knowing where she was going or what she would find when she got there. Either the Indians were fond of Simon or else he didn't have long to live, because they paddled day and night without stopping, relieving each other in the back while one of them caught some sleep in the middle. Sitting in front, Jeanne lamented her lack of experience that rendered her useless.

Fervent prayers rose heavenward. Once again, Honoré Chatel, Mother Berthelet and François were asked to intercede.

"Grandfather, Grandfather, tell God not to call Simon to his hunting paradise right away. Give me a few more years, a few more months. Leave him with me."

When the canoe headed towards the bank of a little river at the end of the afternoon of the second day, there was nothing to indicate the presence of a camp.

The Indian tied the canoe to a branch and made a sign for Jeanne to jump out. In an instant the baggage was unloaded and the large canoe hidden and invisible. As silently as possible, on a thick carpet of dead leaves, the three of them moved into the forest. Weighed down by her bag, which she clutched as if it were a life preserver, Jeanne walked forward like an automaton. In her imagination she had already reached her journey's end, and she had pictured every possibility that might await her so none could disconcert her.

Carrot-Top was blocking the way, but he stood aside and spread the branches. A stream ran between the fir trees. At the foot of a birch stood a shelter made of skins and bark, ten feet long and six feet wide. Nearby was a campfire, the crossed branches above it supporting the iron pot indispensable to all campers.

With a glance, Jeanne asked Carrot-Top the question her

lips did not dare speak. He motioned to the shelter, lifted up the skin door and said simply, "He's waiting for you."

Putting her bag on the ground, Jeanne bent and knelt beside the injured man stretched out on a bed of leaves. She had been prepared for everything except this emaciated, bearded face, these closed eyes sunk into their sockets, this mouth contorted with pain, this rasping, irregular breathing.

Simon was lying on his back. His long thin body, naked to the waist, was covered with an old blanket. His arms were stretched above his head and fastened by the wrists to a leather strap that encircled the trunk of the birch. He turned his head ceaselessly from side to side, and pulled at the bonds tearing into his flesh.

Indignant, Jeanne was already taking out her knife to free him when Carrot-Top, who had squatted down across from her on the other side of Simon, motioned for her to stop.

"It's necessary. Without it, he tears off his bandages in his delirium and hurts himself. Also, often he doesn't recognize me and he attacks me. He's still very strong."

"What's the matter with him?" whispered Jeanne, her heart seized with apprehension.

Carrot-Top pulled back the blanket and uncovered the tanned, emaciated torso. A dirty bandage had been awkwardly wound around the injured man's heaving chest.

"It was an Iroquois ambush," Carrot-Top explained. "They surprised us much farther north. We managed to escape them, but a Huron and Belzile died. Simon got an arrow in his side but he had to run, crawl and paddle for a long time in spite of it. When we were far enough away, I tried to get the arrow out. I didn't succeed. The second time

I tried, he got mad and hit me over the head. Then he asked to be taken south. When we got here, he couldn't go any farther. He said to me, 'Go and get Jeanne.' I didn't dare leave him alone. I sent the Algonquins. That's all there is to tell."

Jeanne was already getting down to work. She took off the bandage stuck to his flesh and asked, "When did it happen?"

"I don't really know."

Carrot-Top was haggard and exhausted, too. "Six days ago, a week. I forget. Maybe less."

Simon groaned and opened his feverish eyes. His pupils were dilated. He gazed at the anxious face bending over him. With effort he spoke in the plaintive voice of those who have suffered greatly and long.

"Jeanne, help me. Jeanne, do something."

The proud man's supplication moved Jeanne even more than the sight of his tortured face. As she would to a sick child, she repeated in a calm, reassuring voice while she examined the horrible wound, "I'm here, Simon. I'm going to cure you. You won't hurt anymore. I'm going to help you. You'll go back home and everything will be fine."

Her laudable optimism was entirely verbal. Her throat tight, she looked at the infected wound from which emerged the broken end of the Iroquois arrow.

Burning with fever, Simon closed his eyes again and turned his head aside.

Should she wait until daylight to remove the projectile that made every breath so painful? When a person is suffering so much, time drags on forever.

Once her resolution was made, Jeanne went into action.

She issued orders and instructions in the spirit of Thérèse de Bretonville.

The three men carried water and set it to boil in the well-scrubbed pot. They doubled the size of the fire, the best source of light. Jeanne inspected her very inadequate instruments. Fortunately, she had the tongs the blacksmith had given her.

A while later she took Carrot-Top aside. His freckled face was pale with emotion.

"Listen, Carrot-Top. You keep talking to me, encourage me, distract me so I won't hear him and so I won't weaken. You know, I'm not a very good healer yet and I'm afraid."

"I understand," Carrot-Top said. His simple soul urged him to take an impulsive action. Squeezing Jeanne's arm, he added confidentially, "The important thing, madame, is that you are here."

The magic phrase that had transformed his life he now offered as a talisman. The two accomplices smiled weakly at each other.

Finally everything was ready. The sides of the tent were rolled up to let in the light and the heat. Two flaming resin torches planted in the ground lit the gloomy scene. Sitting on her heels beside her husband, Jeanne faced the fire. One last time she mentally reviewed everything she would have to do, digging into her memories of Sister Bourgeoys's operation and into her own very inadequate experience. Once she began, she must not hesitate.

Her sleeves were tied up, her hands washed, her instruments laid out beside her. The petticoats cut into bandages were properly rolled. The white thread was there as well as the pine gum gathered during the full moon by old

Hippolyte.

Simon watched these preparations. His pale sea-green eyes were still strangely luminous. Despite his parched lips, he tried to smile, both to give her courage and to ask for it in return.

For the past hour Carrot-Top had been making the injured man swallow mouthfuls of brandy, the remains of the bottle borrowed from the dead man at Quatre-Ruisseaux. Monsieur de Rouville hadn't completely emptied it that day and, like any practical woman, Jeanne had kept it.

The heaviest Algonquin sat on the injured man's legs to hold him down. By his head, kneeling on his outstretched arms, Carrot-Top held the piece of wood he would slip between Simon's teeth as Jeanne had told him to. Even if the firelight indicated their presence, it would be dangerous to tip off potential enemies with screams that could carry very far in the silence of the night.

Jeanne set to work rapidly to shorten her husband's agony. Carrot-Top's voice sustained her, though she did not hear the words he said.

The tongs slipped, slid off the end of the arrow, then took hold again. Calling for strength from heaven, Jeanne pulled with every muscle in her body. Finally, after an eternity of effort, the projectile lodged under the bone in Simon's side was torn from his flesh.

Simon shuddered, writhed, then pushed against the ground, his jaws clamped on the piece of wood. He struggled long, only to collapse into unconsciousness at last, relieving the others as much as himself.

Now he was resting under the wolfskin coat. In the heat

of the fire, his hair was plastered to his forehead, and his breathing was almost imperceptible. Stretched out beside him, Jeanne kept a vigil, attentive to his slightest breath. Her part was done. Providence and nature would do the rest.

For three days and three nights, Monsieur de Rouville was delirious and believed he was a prisoner of the Iroquois. He swore at them, embarrassing Carrot-Top, who blushed crimson. At other times the rough life led by Monsieur de Rouville, trapper and builder, passed before his eyes.

All the solitude and exile of the winters in the forest and the disappointment of his first marriage came out in his wandering speech. The death of Aimée and his baby haunted him.

Jeanne's name recurred constantly. Her undemonstrative husband who did not know how to say "I love you" said it in a hundred different ways, in broken phrases.

When he struggled too much in the bonds they were forced to retighten, Jeanne washed his tormented face and spoke to him gently, as she had to Nicolas during the night they had spent under a tree. Passively, her patient swallowed potions, water or soup, only to vomit them up the next minute. Tireless, Jeanne cleaned him and started all over.

Now and then Carrot-Top made her take a few hours' rest while he did his best to take her place.

On the morning of the fourth day, Simon opened his eyes, turned his head and looked at his wife; she was pale and had circles under her eyes. She was sleeping in a sitting position, her head on her bent knees. Warned by her sixth sense, she, too, opened her eyes and rose painfully to her feet, her back aching.

A ghost of his authoritarian voice ordered, "Go get some sleep right now. And untie me. I won't run away."

Simon was on the road to recovery. He was making rapid progress.

At the end of the week, the council of war from which Simon was excluded but which he dominated with his orders and advice, decided to return as quickly as possible to civilization before the cold and ice forced them to winter on the spot.

Stretched out in the bottom of the canoe, his head on Jeanne's lap, Simon either slept soundly or demanded to be told stories he only half listened to.

"I'm wasting my time," Jeanne finally burst out impatiently when he closed his eyes at the best part of her story of the "Knight of Azur."

A blissful smile spread over Simon's face, pale under his tan. He assured her, "Not at all, go on. It's not the story that particularly interests me. It's your voice and your choice of words."

"Isn't my choice of words right?"

"It's adorable, just like you, scholarly and down-to-earth at the same time. What did the poor knight of Azur do when his girlfriend slammed the door of the chateau?"

Resigned, the storyteller took up her tale as she combed her husband's short black beard with her fingers. It made him look like a pirate of the high seas. After five minutes, she fell silent. He was sleeping, and his hand, like Isabelle's in her sleep, was clinging fast to the king's daughter's fingers.

34

SIMON'S convalescence began with the first snow; he was making progress and getting worse at the same time. As he recovered his strength, the little house seemed to grow smaller. Soon Jeanne, exasperated, had the feeling the walls were about to burst from holding in so much energy under pressure.

To restore her patience while Simon grumbled against the cold, the snow, the logs in the fireplace and the heat, the mistress of the house hummed absent-mindedly:

Lui y a longtemps que je t'aime,
Jamais je ne t'oublierai...

An unexpected silence made her look up. Simon was sitting up in bed, his back against the wall, staring at her severely.

"What's the matter now? Am I singing off-key?"

"Off-key wouldn't matter. The song itself worries me."

Too late, Jeanne realized that, for a few moments, she had become Jean Chatel again, the boy with the big ears who had learned much on his travels.

"Come over here right now and tell me how a lady like you could have heard—and most of all remembered—those verses. Forget that endless mending and sit here beside me. A husband has serious responsibilities, even if he is a cripple."

210

Falsely submissive, Jeanne set her work aside. Through the window she spied Nicolas and Isabelle riding down the slope on their crude toboggan, Miraud chasing them. She settled down on the bed beside Simon, her head on his left shoulder to avoid the still-sensitive scar.

Monsieur de Rouville declared anxiously, "I cannot permit that kind of language under a roof that shelters a king's daughter. And what will our future son say when he hears his mother singing like that?"

"It will be a girl, and you know it. She'll think I've got a lot of spirit to sing in these conditions, with a husband like you within earshot to tell me what to do every step of the way. Come on. Put on your coat. We're going for a walk in the snow. You're pampering yourself."

That was the most beautiful Christmas in the twenty years of Jeanne Chatel de Rouville's eventful life.

Simon gave her a cradle he thought he had built without her knowing. She presented him with a fringed shirt she had made while he was taking his naps. Indiscreetly, he had kept his eyes half-open, secretly admiring her.

Nicolas and Isabelle solemnly recited the poems their mother had patiently taught them, and that their father had heard them stumble through a thousand times.

Miraud and the cat, side by side, warmed themselves in front of the fire.

Carrot-Top, Mathurin, Gansagonas and even the two Hurons, attracted by so much happiness and warmth, shared in the feast served on wooden plates. The little house nestled in the snow rang with laughter and song. Through the glass window, a ray of golden light spread its cheerful message onto the snow.

35

JEANNE and Mathurin were notching the maple trees as they tried to predict the quantity of sugar they would produce this time. It was a good year for sap.

"It's a good year for everything," Jeanne decided. "Simon has recovered, Nicolas knows how to read, Isabelle doesn't suck her thumb anymore, and I'm expecting a baby."

Not to be left out, Limp added to the happy litany. "Miraud no longer chases rabbits. Gansagonas cured my rheumatism...in my legs, at least. My arm will need more poultices."

Nicolas, who was carving the wooden pegs that would be stuck into the trunks, got into the act. "There are no more stones in the garden. Papa and Carrot-Top are going to bring back a lot of furs, even if they started too late. And Mama will have another boy."

"I haven't fallen into the water yet with my new fur-lined coat, and Mama will have another girl," Isabelle added to this enumeration of good things.

Miraud stood up and turned towards the river. Was it visitors... or was it Father returning sooner than expected?

Everyone ran to the river bank, full of anticipation. Two canoes were passing, rapid and silent, full to the water line with people. Their frightened eyes glanced at the intrigued spectators without seeing them.

A third craft slowed down for a moment. Jeanne recognized the Bibeau family whose daughter had married the summer before.

Without raising his voice, the father said, "Iroquois. They're everywhere. Run. They're following us."

His wife hushed him, thinking only of herself in her terror.

"Don't waste time. Quick. Keep going. They're going to catch us. They're right behind."

The Bibeaus hastened away in a panic.

Jeanne looked at Mathurin, her face ghastly pale. Miraud growled, his hackles raised, trembling with rage. She put her hand around his muzzle and whispered an order. "Children, lie down under the canoe. Don't move."

She pulled the dog with her behind a bush. Limp was already stretched out on the ground, his musket in front of him.

Four Iroquois appeared at the bend in the river, hunched over their paddles. Two other canoes followed right behind them. Almost crushed by Jeanne, Miraud was strangling in silent rage.

Without a glance at the whites crouched on the river bank, the Indians disappeared, gaining ground on their victims.

Motionless, the group waited. Ten minutes passed with no change. Cautiously Jeanne released the dog, who didn't make a move. For the time being, there were no enemies in sight.

Mathurin motioned at the canoe with his chin. "Should we go?"

Jeanne held her head in both hands to think things over better. She had already made a hundred different plans in anticipation of this type of situation. Which of all those plans was the best one now?

"No. Not the canoe. They're ahead and behind. Let's stay here."

"We can't take to the woods, that's for sure. They'll come that way, too."

"Quick, children. Go to the house."

Gansagonas appeared on the doorstep. She was holding a heavy sack of provisions. Wise and confident, she already knew which of the alternatives was preferable.

She set down the sack and went in to prepare another one. In a voice that Simon the despot would not approve of, Jeanne announced, "Limp, I'm taking the family into the cellar. What will you do?"

"I'll stay hidden in the bushes by the water. Anonkade will be coming back from fishing a few hours from now. He and his friend will help us."

"And the dog?"

Jeanne and Mathurin understood each other at a glance. They could not risk Miraud betraying his masters' hide-out in his eagerness to protect them.

"I'll take the dog with me," the old hunter decided, his hand on his knife, nodding to his mistress.

Poor Miraud, thought Jeanne. Then an instant later she added, Poor us.

"Quick, children. Follow me. We're going to play hiding in the cellar, like we practised."

The mother partridge's trick vaguely combined with the Trojan horse strategy had inspired the astute king's daughter to devise a possible way to outwit the enemy.

Until now, the whites had opposed the Iroquois attacks either with a desperate resistance or an even more disastrous retreat. The cellar Simon had dug for his fur pelts had been enlarged, improved and cleaned up by Jeanne and Gansagonas. This unexpected use it had been put to offered a slim chance for safety.

"Will we make a snack like last time?" asked Isabelle. She had pleasant memories of the exercises they had practised many times since their father's departure.

"Yes. Perhaps several."

"Will we have light?" asked Nicolas anxiously. Since his fall in the ravine, darkness still held danger for him.

"Gansagonas will be there, and so will I. Quickly, climb down."

She carefully set the turf aside, uncovering the square trap door. A rough ladder plunged into the darkness. Nicolas hesitated. Jeanne gave him a push.

"There's a candle down there and a flint stone. Light it for me as I showed you."

Very proud, the boy conquered his fear and climbed agilely down the ladder. Isabelle burst into tears.

"Where's Zeanne? She's going to want to come."

"I'll bring her to you in a little while. Jump."

Kneeling at the edge of the hole, Jeanne grasped Isabelle by the wrists, swung her into the emptiness and dropped her a foot from the bottom. An instant later, the little girl, who took after her father, began showering her brother with advice as he did his utmost to produce a spark.

It was cold and damp in that low cellar, dug right into the earth. Fur pelts, the relics of Simon's first disastrous expedition before Christmas, were waiting to be packed in bales. An odour of wild beasts filled the confined space.

Gansagonas, the expression on her face carefully impassive, yet with bright eyes, arrived with gourds of water, sacks, blankets and clothing. She disappeared into the cellar without a word. It was the second time she had faced the Iroquois with the children. During the last raid, she had had time to flee into the forest while men burned down the house, scalped her mistress and killed the baby in her arms.

This time she was only too happy to let the determined white woman make the decisions.

Jeanne said, "I'm closing up the trap door. Barricade it from inside. Open it when I knock twice. You know what to give the children."

Without discussion, Gansagonas pulled the trap door shut. As luck would have it, Nicolas managed to light the candle that very moment. The first minutes would not be too difficult. Jeanne replaced the turf that Simon had artfully cut. No one would guess the hiding place. Now it was time to set the scene Jeanne had planned. With her fertile imagination and sense for the practical, she had considered every aspect of the problem that might arise. Now she would have liked to discuss the plan with Simon. If only she had time to carry it out before the Iroquois arrived.

Jeanne was as active and sure in danger as she was awkward and clumsy in the public eye or in household chores. Like a hurricane unleashed, she was everywhere.

From her trunk, she took the long hair she had cut off the summer before. She ran down to the river and hung it on a branch where it could be easily seen.

With one kick she smashed in the bark canoe and

216

pushed it towards deep water, where it slowly sank. The paddles she threw into the river drifted down the current, turning circles.

"Good luck, Limp," she called towards the bushes. She felt the old hunter's presence there, though she could not see him. Miraud whimpered. He wanted so much to come to her. As long as there was hope, Mathurin would spare the dog that had become his hunting companion. But you couldn't risk that many lives to save an animal. As soon as he sounded the alarm, he would have to be killed.

Jeanne picked up her skirts in an impatient and characteristic gesture. She galloped towards the house and leaned her musket near the door. She quickly slipped on her "brother's" suit and fastened the belt around her waist; it would scarcely go around her once. Would this baby they'd waited for so long and hoped for so much ever have the chance to see the light of day? She made sure she had everything she needed: the knife Charron had given her, the powder horn, the bag of lead shot.

Jeanne grabbed the container of sea-wolf oil, the lamp fuel she had traded some maple sugar for. She spread the viscous liquid over the table, the floor, under the bed. The beautiful patchwork comforter went to join the grey cape, the wolfskin coat and Zeanne the doll near the door.

Had she forgotten anything? She went through the cabin to check. Oh, yes! The flowered sugar bowl Thérèse de Bretonville had given to Isabelle. It still contained some dry maple sugar that Nicolas had pounded into a powder.

A shot rang out by the river; Mathurin's hopeless battle had begun. The Iroquois had come too soon. She wouldn't have time to carry out her clever plan. Under no pretext would she go near the trap door of the cellar. The mother partridge does not betray her young.

A shadow blocked the light outlined by the door. An Iroquois was there, his face painted, threatening, tomahawk in hand.

He didn't seem to be in a hurry and he was alone. A glance through the window—her beautiful, precious window—assured her of that. A small canoe was drawn up on the bank. The Iroquois always travelled in twos in these craft. Was it this one's companion Mathurin had fired at? Why wasn't he firing any more shots?

All these unanswered questions jostled together in Jeanne's head. On the threshold, the Indian had not moved. He was studying her at length, intrigued by her unexpected reaction. Usually white women screamed, went into hysterics or fainted. This one was eyeing him calmly and walking towards the hearth, without letting go of her sugar bowl.

She bent down, picked up a log with one end still smoking and shook it in the embers to ignite it again. Then she calmly directed it towards the table glistening with oil.

With a low rumble, the fire covered it and reached towards the ceiling. The Iroquois let out a cry of rage and rushed forward, raising his axe. The madwoman had no right to light the fire herself without giving him time to choose his trophies.

The poacher's granddaughter had carried around mustard powder for too many years during her youth not to be ready to use it. Instinctively, with a snap of her wrist, she threw the contents of the sugar bowl in the Indian's face. The large pieces of brown sugar didn't affect him, but the powder that Nicolas had carefully ground with his pestle filled the startled man's eyes. He put both his hands to his face, the same reflex Thierry had had long before. Then that familiar rage took hold of Jeanne at the sight of this brute who dared invade her home and endanger her family.

Her fingers closed around the long handle of the cast-iron frying pan. She raised it, and with all the strength of her anger, crashed it down on the bent head. The Indian collapsed in a heap. The greedy flames licked the walls, reached the other puddles of oil and leaped in their infernal dance.

Jeanne shook herself and ran towards the door before the fire cut off her retreat. On the way she tripped over the pile of clothing she'd thrown there earlier. She grabbed her musket as she kicked the coat, cape, coverlet and doll outside. Possessions were so scarce in New France that everyone was attached to them, even in the gravest danger.

Jeanne glanced around to make sure no other enemy was in sight. Did she have time to get rid of the Iroquois's canoe? That was a necessity, for without it, the scene she'd set would be useless.

The next Iroquois who passed by must see the smoking ruins and the head of hair that would tell the triumphant story of scalpings and murders. They would continue on their way, searching for other prey their brother had not yet reached.

This second trip to the river demanded more of Jeanne than all her previous acts. She was drained of all her rage and courage. She had but one thought: to dive into the safety of the cellar. For an instant she hesitated.

Yet finally she ran towards the water. A vigorous push sent the light canoe into the midst of the current, and it

219

went off on its own, carried away on the river swollen by the spring thaw.

Very softly she called, "Mathurin?"

No one answered. She dashed into the bushes where the trapper had been hiding without even the most elementary caution. The courageous mother was no more than an automaton, and it was better that way. With no horror, no reaction, she contemplated the body of the dog with its throat slit at her feet. Farther away was an Indian who must have been killed almost at point-blank range by Limp, since his tomahawk had had time to split open the old coureur de bois's bald head.

Jeanne let the branches close again over the spectacle that she would relive in her nightmares. She raced back towards the house that was blazing briskly, her beautiful chateau in the forest. With a sharp crack, the window shattered.

Unfolding the comforter, she piled up the clothes, Zeanne and even the cat that had scampered over to her, returning from a fruitful hunt.

Two sharp knocks. The trap door opened. The candle flickered. It wasn't so cold; the bodies huddled together warmed the shelter. On the other hand, the atmosphere was already heavy. Would the air holes the two women had provided be sufficient? Jeanne had prescribed a strong dose of paregoric that Gansagonas prepared for the children. They had swallowed it and were now sleeping soundly.

They had to be spared the horror of waiting in the darkness; they must not be given the chance to cry or raise their voices.

Carefully, Jeanne lowered the trap door. The turf was in its proper place. In the "rehearsals," it fit perfectly with the grass around it.

"Grandfather, take care of everything for me. You can see it from up there. Hide us well."

Jeanne quickly told her Huron companion about the latest events. Together they took silent inventory of their riches. The water would have to be rationed.

The children were stretched out on the unrolled furs, and Jeanne covered them with her cape. Then she wrapped the wolfskin coat around her; if she survived, her baby should not be made to suffer from her carelessness. She smiled at the tardiness of her concern.

Jeanne stretched out next to the children, placed the flint stone and her musket beside her and stuck her dagger into the earthen floor as Simon did. The food was piled close by and the water was not far. A final wave of her hand to Gansagonas; the Indian nodded her head. Then Jeanne blew out the candle. Like a presence, the darkness surrounded and crushed them. The interminable vigil began. Fortunately the children were sleeping, and as soon as they woke up, they would be given something to eat and another potion to swallow. The cat purred at Jeanne's feet, the only symbol of life in that frigid tomb.

"Grandfather, Mother Berthelet, François, I love you very much, but don't expect me right away, for pity's sake. I still have so many things to do, so many people to love. Simon, where are you? Simon, if you come to my aid, watch out for the Iroquois. What good would it do for me to get out of here alive if you're not waiting for me in the sunshine?

"Simon, our son will have your eyes. We'll build our house again. Simon, we'll be happy. I want us to be happy."

36

INCH by inch, very carefully, the trap door was lifted. It was light. The time was still not right.

Silence. Waiting. Her straining ears heard only silence and more silence. The cat's purring had become maddening. It echoed and reverberated and seemed to come from everywhere at once.

Was it better to sleep and dream, or to stay awake and imagine? Was it time for a new attempt? A breath of fresh air cautiously filtered in and hit her full in the face, making her dizzy, almost forcing her to let go of the ladder. Was it dark, or did her eyes, too accustomed to blackness, no longer know how to see?

Carried by the wind, the acrid odour of the fire caught in her throat.

By lifting the trap door, she could see in front and to the sides. Perhaps the enemy was behind, crouching there for hours, waiting with the infinite patience of the Indian for the victim to fall into his trap. So much the worse. She had to know.

Three days and as many nights had passed, maybe more. She had to get a change of scenery; she had to breathe. If necessary, she would dive back into the shadows.

Silence. Night noises. The cicadas, the frogs. The soft

moon silvered the foot of the trees.

No more house before her. Blackened beams in the sky. The chimney standing. Simon's chimneys don't fall down. They remain, like monuments to bereavements. They will have to sweep all that, rebuild, live again in the light.

Were there carefree people who dared to go out into the sunlight, to lift their voices, to laugh in its brightness?

The raised trap door allowed young Madame de Rouville to come out, little belly and all. Nothing behind? Nothing in front?

Her nose in the grass, how good it was to smell the night. Mathurin had his nose in the grass, too, and a hatchet in his skull. Poor Mathurin. Poor Miraud. Poor Simon and Jeanne's house.

Come now, buck up. This was meant to be an exploration. All right, then. Explore.

It was less dangerous on all fours. It was easier, too. It was even necessary since the stiff-limbed troglodytes no longer knew how to walk. What a lovely word Grandfather had taught her: troglodyte. Simon would laugh when he heard her say it.

Could Simon still laugh?

What was that noise? Now it was too late to return to the trap door. The mother partridge does not betray her young.

Someone was talking. Who dared to speak in front of the ruined house? Two men. Two shadows sitting on the blackened doorstep. She had to get away, lead the enemy far from her young partridges, towards the river.

Slowly, gently.

The men were talking. An indistinct murmur. Here was the sand under her hands and knees. And the bush where

223

Mathurin was sleeping, his nose in the hay.

There were two canoes on the bank. Had her trick not completely succeeded? The Iroquois had stopped. They were waiting, in spite of everything.

One of them called out. He said, "Are you coming, Rouville?"

A sigh answered him, coming from very close, from the shore.

Iroquois don't speak French, don't say, "Are you coming, Rouville?"

In the moonlight a man was kneeling on the ground, his shoulders bent. He was running his fingers through the long hair he had taken from the branch where it had been hanging.

Iroquois don't cry softly, repeating, "Jeanne, my Jeanne."

It's funny, that story about the Iroquois, the cat, and the dog, and the hair...I'll have to tell it to Simon; he won't listen all the way through. The earth is turning so much I'm dizzy.

Suddenly the man stood up. His knife was gleaming in his hand. He moved soundlessly. The hair was hanging from his left hand.

Hair doesn't grow on your hand. How tall and silent he is. Is he a shadow? A dream like the others, or a nightmare?

The dagger was shining in the moonlight as it shone in the sunshine another time...another...another time...

Now I don't have to wake up because the dream is marvellous.

Strong arms, warm lips, a voice reverberating and repeating the same thing a hundred times. I'll have to sleep again, for a long time, to dream of Simon who's cradling me and crying in my hair. The hair on my head, not the hair on the tree.

I have to tell him the children are sleeping under the earth. Simon will be happy...he'll laugh and build a beautiful house...he'll stop shouting, "Charron, Carrot-Top. She's here. Jeanne is here. They're safe."

We'll need a new cradle for the green-eyed baby...and a cradle for Zeanne...and a new dog...another frying pan to hit the Iroquois over the head with...there will be an army of the king's daughters brandishing frying pans...we'll need a sugar bowl for the mustard...why those fingers on my lips? I can talk for five hours at a time. I did it once before. But no one was kissing me to make me quiet. No one was holding me so tight I was suffocating.

When I wake up, I'll tell all that to Simon. I'll lose myself in his eyes as pale as light.

37

VILLE-MARIE, *August, 1674*

> *Dear Marie,*
> *Not one year but two have gone by since I gave this yellowed notebook to Mademoiselle Crolo. In it I find my anxieties as a young bride and my promise of an epilogue. Here it is. This evening some voyageurs are leaving for Quebec to trade the northern trappers' furs. They will bring you this tale.*

Jeanne raised her head and contemplated the river flowing by the window where she sat. For two days she and her little family had been the guests of Sister Bourgeoys at Pointe Saint-Charles. The founder had bought the Saint-Gabriel farm; it now sheltered her live-in students and king's daughters who were learning how to keep house as they awaited their husbands.

The congregation sisters, several of whom were novices who had come over with Jeanne Chatel, took possession of the children and spoiled them outrageously. Cries of delight were heard coming from the dairy. Isabelle and Nicolas had never seen a cow being milked, and the sight enchanted them.

Lost in thought, Jeanne leaned her elbows on the little rickety table a grateful soldier had built for Sister Bourgeoys. How could she express all the happiness her joyful heart contained on a piece of paper?

Where can I begin? Jeanne wondered. If I could talk to her in person, it would be so much easier. I've always been known for my dramatic tales. This paper paralyzes me. She dipped her pen resolutely into the ink and in a firm hand wrote:

I was afraid I'd be a poor replacement for you at Monsieur de Rouville's side, you who are so pretty and gentle.

In the end, it was much better that I became his wife instead of you. How can I say that politely?

I dreaded his dead wife's ghost. I looked too much like her.

How many misunderstandings there had been because of that unfortunate coincidence!

I had no need to fear poor Aimée's memory.

She faded away in death as she had in life, a sad, fearful little shadow. It wouldn't be very tactful to mention that.

The pale, frightened children broke my heart when they called me "Mama."

Now they'd break my heart every bit as much if they didn't call me that. But in spite of it all, I do appreciate this time off, when I hear them just at a distance.

Simon has been bustling around the town since morning, meeting his friends. How can I describe my husband to Marie?

If I tell her he's tall and tanned, with sparkling white teeth and extraordinary eyes, she'll think I'm exaggerating as usual. And that description might make her think her own husband, that nice little Lieutenant Dauvergne, is colour-

227

less and commonplace.

Should I admit to her that my lord is authoritarian, blunt and given to mockery? That he bullies me without thinking twice, treats me cavalierly and expects me to understand everything instinctively? My poor friend would think I have an unhappy marriage with a brute lacking in all refinement.

Jeanne, still lost in her thoughts, chewed on her goose feather pen without deriving any inspiration from it. She continued, searching for words:

Your cousin Simon de Rouville is exactly the kind of husband I needed, the very opposite of the ideal we used to dream of long ago. That proves romantic young girls don't know what's right for them.

I saw our Thierry with the white horse again. He's wandering through the forests of Canada pursuing his dream of freedom.

We live in a cabin in the middle of the woods; it's barely big enough to contain our happiness.

I wouldn't dare say that I set fire to it myself. She'd think it was out of carelessness.

We are just finishing building our new house. It will be magnificent.

Preoccupied, Jeanne pictured it. She saw the log house that Simon, Carrot-Top and Charron had built on the blackened ruins. Two chimneys, two rooms, an attic and three glass windows—an unheard-of luxury. Even if she listed all that, Marie, who lived in town, wouldn't have the proper idea of the splendour of their second residence. Too bad!

The nuns in Troyes would be proud of me. Here I am, a

decent housewife who can handle a needle, a broom and especially a frying pan, all with ease.

Hmm! A little too well, perhaps. Oh, well, let's get on with it.

Jeanne sighed, exasperated. So many things in her daily life would seem unthinkable to her peaceable friend. Jeanne reread what she had written and frowned.

It's time I described my life a little, and set myself off to advantage. If I don't, Marie won't recognize me.

Her pen flew across the paper.

We were isolated by the snow for months, shut up for days at a time. Simon hunted, set traps and collected furs. I made warm clothing from them, under the direction of an Indian woman, and the children would come inside with their cheeks pink from the cold. I got used to living with a musket over my shoulder, never venturing more than a hundred feet from the house. I learned some essential things they didn't teach us in the convent: how to fashion snowshoes and moccasins, make tea from spruce bark to guard against scurvy, boil roots to combat fever and rub noses with snow to unfreeze them. I know how to prepare pemmican, light a fire from green wood and tan hides and gather wild honey.

I became a healer and people come from far away to see me. It's my way of repaying for all I've taken from life.

It's also an excellent way to get rare commodities, but if I say that, I'll seem mercenary.

We have known cold and hunger as well. But for the first time in my life I am happy, flowering, useful and, I really must say...in love.

My trousseau is scattering in all directions. I made myself a dress of soft leather, like the Hurons wear. I wear moccasins all the time. My skin is tanned, my face has filled out and my eyes shine. When I look at myself in the river water, I think I'm almost pretty. Simon calls me his otter when he strokes my hair.

Jeanne caught herself dreaming, a smile on her face. She gave herself a shake and went on with her epistle.

Our daughter was born in the spring in a tent made of skins. Her name is Honorine, in memory of my grandfather. She has green eyes like her father.

Jeanne sighed. Marie couldn't possibly guess how difficult it was to stand up to those green eyes. You had to be surrounded by them to understand.

It would be premature to announce that our next son will be called François and the third, Thierry, she thought.

When we have another daughter, she will be baptized Marie, in honour of you.

And the next ones will be Marguerite, Anne and Geneviève. Oh, I've got a lot of work ahead of me.

The sun was setting on the horizon. Simon would appear soon, hurrying along to wreak havoc on the peaceful farm and make the busy sisters blush and laugh.

He would admire her chaste white cap and high, immaculately clean collar and whisper in her ears, "Madame de Rouville, that looks splendid on you."

At the same time, he'd pinch her on the behind or slip his arm around her waist when no one was looking.

She had to finish this letter as soon as possible. Her pen took flight again, which did not improve her untidy handwriting.

Life here is always at the mercy of the Iroquois. Every year the Five Nations become more threatening. The weight of this uncertainty crushes some and seems to give others the need to live more intensely.

I am of the latter. I count the hours of my happy life as a miser counts his treasure.

I am told your husband is prospering in his father's business, but that you wish to return to France to live. Wherever you go, Marie, my gratitude will go with you.

I'll end this notebook by thanking you for having made my happiness.

Tomorrow we will return to our house in the forest. It is my chateau, on my lord's estate. Surrounded by my children, I will live and die there as a king's daughter.

Your friend forever and always,
Jeanne Chatel de Rouville

It was time. At the end of the road, Simon was coming. He was walking along, Isabelle perched on his shoulders. Nicolas, proudly weighed down with the heavy musket, was stretching his little legs to keep up with his father.

Then came that strong voice that asked impatiently, "Where is your baby sister? And what did your remarkable mother do today?"

PUBLISHER'S NOTE
TO THE READER

The King's Daughter was first published in 1974; the first English edition was published in 1980. When the book was written and translated into English, a number of terms were used to describe native people which today are considered offensive. In this new edition we have tried to remove that offensive language.

The book describes the experiences of a young woman who was sent to Canada from an orphanage in France, in order to become a wife to a widowed French coureur de bois. Many young French girls came to this country under these circumstances.

Because the book is written from Jeanne Chatel's point of view, there are many scenes in which she is frightened by the wilderness around her, by the rough French hunters and woodsmen she meets, and by the native people in whose country she finds herself. This book does not claim to present a true picture of the First Peoples who were living in what is now Quebec at that time. But it does show us how the world might have seemed to a young European woman.